BOLTS OF THUNDER

THUNDER

WORDS OF

WHISPER

To Marty

Best wishes

BY

JAMES VINCENT POWERS

James Vincent Powers

First published by Dog Ear Publishing
4010 W. 86th Street, Ste H
Indianapolis, IN 46268
www.dogearpublishing.net

ISBN: 978-159858-955-9

Printed in the United States of America

Acknowledgments

I'm deeply grateful to the pilots of the 511th Fighter Squadron whose friendship and encounters will never be forgotten. I also thank Paul Powers for his unending technical support, Lois Rupprecht for her outstanding editing and continuous encouragement, and Victory Crayne and Melody Shore for their many valuable critiques.

Special thanks go to Kay Siering of the German Spiegl Television Company, who was instrumental in my being involved with the recovery of the P-47 airplane in Austria and my appearing in the resulting films that were played in Germany, Austria and the United States.

Prologue

(France, October 1944)

"Will this be the day I die?"

Mark Andrews looked intently through his canopy at the planes taxiing into position in front of him, and nervously waited his turn. He again scrutinized his instrument panel and made sure that each of his gauges were in the green. He readjusted his trim tabs. His tension was building, and he started to break out into a sweat. The P-47 Thunderbolt was a one-man fighter, and he and he alone was responsible for its performance. He watched each plane accelerate down the slushy runway in turn, splashing melting snow in arcs of ice water from their speeding wheels. Their powerful engines lifted them off as they climbed to join the circling squadron. Being the squadron's newest pilot, he would be the last to take off.

Mark felt both excited and frightened as he waited. Just a little over a year and a half ago, he had been a business correspondent for a chemical company in Louisville, Kentucky, and had never flown an airplane. Now he was waiting in line to face the most formidable enemy the world had ever known: Adolf Hitler's Luftwaffe.

He had many questions that he could have—should have—asked his instructors and the other pilots in the squadron. But even before joining the Army Air Corps, whenever he asked a soldier, "What's it like in the military service?" the answer was usually evasive, "You'll find out." He finally concluded that maybe the service was different things to different people, and maybe that's what made it hard to explain those experiences to others.

Mark's muscles tightened as he watched his element leader, Lieutenant Martin, start to pull onto the runway. Mark eased his throttle forward and followed slightly behind and to the right of him. Without further hesitation, they pushed their throttles full forward to start their take-off roll. The engines roared as they accelerated down the runway. As they felt their wheels leave the ground, they made a steep, climbing turn to join the other two planes in their group, Blue Flight. The four of them climbed to slide into formation with the squadron's other two flights. The twelve planes continued climbing as they headed toward the front lines.

Mark felt he knew his airplane like an old friend, but now that they were going to cross into enemy-held territory, he realized how much his life hinged on the continued operation of its one engine. He leaned forward in the cockpit and strained to listen. It seemed that he could hear each piston as it fired. Did one misfire? Was the engine running a bit rough? He listened again. No, it was purring smoothly.

They continued their climb as they crossed the front lines. Not a word had been spoken among the pilots since leaving their briefing that morning. They maintained radio silence as long as possible, so as not to give away their position.

As a wingman, Mark watched intently for enemy aircraft. He started at the left side of the canopy, swept his eyes slowly across the sky, then scanned his instrument panel, and continued out through the right side of the canopy. He repeated the process from right to left—all the time while flying a fairly tight formation on his element leader's wing—who was flying his slot in the flight, which was, in turn, flying its slot in the squadron formation.

They leveled off at twenty-five thousand feet as they approached the target area.

Mark was glad to be flying the Air Corps' newest, and what he felt was their best, fighter plane, the P-47 Thunderbolt. It was a rugged plane that could take a lot of punishment. He was sure of that because he had just walked away after crashing one two days before. They carried two, 500-pound bombs, one under each wing, and four, 50-caliber machine guns in each wing.

As they approached the target area, the squadron started to go into a slow left turn.

Suddenly their radio silence was broken by his squadron commander's voice. "Browning Squadron, there's our target below, the railroad marshalling yard. Red Flight will hit the rails at the north end of the yard. White Flight hit the south end. Blue Flight will get the round house and the multiple tracks in between."

Instantly, the sky became filled with the ominous black puffs of smoke created by exploding antiaircraft fire scattering around and between them. This was the big stuff, German "88s," the deadly, large 88 mm antiaircraft cannons.

Mark shivered and couldn't help thinking it was really like Russian roulette with the shells bursting randomly around him. The next one could explode where his plane was just as easily as a hundred yards to the right or left.

They started jinking by changing altitude and direction slightly as they circled the target area, in an effort to confuse the antiaircraft computers.

"Okay, Red Flight, let's go."

Mark looked down at the target and was startled by all the small-caliber antiaircraft guns which were firing below. They produced a smaller burst of white smoke than the big black bursts of the 88 mm cannons that were reaching their altitude. So many light shells were being fired that they formed a thin, white cloud layer at around twelve thousand feet.

Mark watched in awe as the first flight peeled off, rolled into a steep wingover, and entered their dive. Each plane followed the one before it at five-second intervals. Mark looked down and watched in amazement as the squadron commander dove headlong into the cloud layer of flak. He can't fly through that, Mark thought. He'll be shot down for sure. The squadron commander's plane penetrated the cloud, followed by the second, third, and fourth fighters.

They're all going to get shot down, he thought. No one can possibly survive all that flak.

But as he looked, the first plane pulled up through the layer, then the second, but as the third Thunderbolt started its climb, it got hit in the right wing and started cartwheeling wildly. Mark watched it disappear back through the layer. Then the cloud lit up with an orange glow as the plane hit the ground and exploded. When the fourth fighter completed his climb into position, the commanding officer's voice came through again.

"White Flight—your turn."

Mark watched again as the next flight peeled off and repeated the unbelievable drama.

The four planes successfully released their bombs and emerged from the bowels of the inferno below. It seemed to take such a long time, as if it were all happening in slow motion.

Mark kept wishing they would hurry up so they could get out of there. After all, how many times can they keep shooting at me and missing? he thought.

His thoughts were suddenly shattered as the squadron leader's voice came over the air again.

"Okay, Blue Flight, it's your turn!"

Oh wow, this is it.

He watched his flight leader go into his dive. Mark waited five seconds, then rolled over almost onto his back, pulled his nose down through the horizon, watching as his gun sight passed through the patchwork landscape of the farms and forests, finally stopping on the town below. He adjusted his dive to place his sight on the rail yard. He reached over and pulled the handle that armed his two, 500- pound bombs.

He was picking up speed fast, and quickly yanked the right handle to release his bombs. The handle wouldn't budge!

His airspeed had been building rapidly, and he had very little time before he had to start his pull-up to keep from diving into the ground. He was getting desperate. He had to get rid of his bombs. He tried with all his might to pull the release handle, but it still would not budge.

He let go of the stick and clamped it between his knees, and reached across to his right so that he could pull the handle with both hands. There was a small grunting sound, and then he felt the handle move. His bombs were released.

Where they landed was hard to say. Because of his gyrations in the cockpit, the gun sight had wandered quite a bit from his target, the railroad yard, and out into the fields surrounding the town. Some farmer would probably find two big craters in his crop after they had gone.

Mark had penetrated the cloud of small-arms fire, successfully going down. Now he had to pull his plane back up and go through it again. Somehow, he made it through and was able to join the rest of the squadron. As he leveled off and reentered the formation, their leader turned away from the target area, and led them back home.

They landed on their partly snow-covered field and parked their planes. Several jeeps came around to pick up the pilots and take them on a cold, bumpy ride back to the ready room for their debriefing.

They learned that the missing pilot was Lt. Shelly, one of the new pilots who had joined the squadron the same time as Mark. He had seemed like a nice guy and Mark had hoped they could become good friends. It was a strange feeling to realize that he was gone forever. He wondered how many people back home would be affected by his death.

* * * *

The intelligence officer listened as the pilots told him where their bombs had hit. Needless to say, Mark did not have much to offer.

A few days later, however, they got electric bomb releases, and he never had that problem again.

Mark also discussed the flight with Lt. Martin.

"I'm surprised we didn't see any enemy aircraft," Mark remarked."Don't get too anxious, Mark. You'll see them soon enough."

CHAPTER 1

(Alabama; Mississippi)

Mark learned to fly in the U.S. Army Air Corps.

His class had just finished two months of rigorous physical and academic training in preflight school at Montgomery, Alabama. Now as a student pilot, he was no longer called a private, but referred to as a cadet. He was given a different insignia consisting of wings with a propeller in the middle which he wore on the collar of his uniform, and a larger one which he wore on his hat.

The cadets were all eagerly looking forward to their next step, which was primary flying school, where they would actually fly their first airplanes.

They all ran to see the announcement posted on the bulletin board which told them where they were going to be sent. Some were going to Florida, some to Georgia. Mark was on a list of twenty-five cadets going to Jackson, Mississippi.

"Mississippi!" some of the fellows said, "Mississippi is the worst place in the world you could go. The heat is sweltering, and the swamps are so bad that if you had to parachute out of your plane and land in one, the snakes and alligators would eat you alive before you could be rescued."

With that thought in mind, Mark boarded the troop train and went to Jackson with 24 other cadets.

* * * *

The war in Europe seemed to be finally turning more favorable for the Allies. They had invaded Sicily and were entrenched in southern Italy, attempting to move northward but meeting strong resistance. The British and American air forces started making air raids into Germany from Britain. However, Germany still occupied all of France, Belgium, Holland, Denmark and Norway.

* * * *

(Mississippi)

Mark's train arrived in Jackson. His group was loaded onto a bus and driven into the countryside about fifteen miles north of town. They turned off the main highway and traveled along a winding, picturesque, country road. As they rounded a bend, they were greeted with a sight that could have been a scene from a World War I movie.

A bi-winged airplane had just taken off from a grassy field and was making a climbing turn as it cleared some graceful, billowy trees. It continued its climb until it was out of view.

As their bus continued down the road, they could see the small airfield that the plane had taken off from. It had a neatly-painted, white rail fence around its perimeter, and a hangar at one end. Several bi-winged Stearman airplanes were busily taking off and landing, yet they somehow blended in with the languid and peaceful feeling of their surroundings. Other similar airplanes were parked in two rows in front of the hangar, patiently awaiting their pilots.

On the other side of the road, several long, white cabins were nestled at the edge of a wooded grove and surrounded by another white fence. The feeling was that of a pleasant rest camp. The bus turned in the gate and pulled up to a stop alongside one of the cabins. They were told by the driver that this would be their barracks while they were at primary flying school.

The next morning, they were taken across the road to a one-story wooden building near the hangar. This was to be their flight planning and briefing room, which they would refer to as the "ready room." Here the new cadets were introduced to their instructors. Mark's instructor was named Mr. Baxter. Mr. Baxter appeared to be in his late twenties, which seemed old in contrast to most of the teenage student pilots. One could tell right off that he was a rather serious person, and that there would be no fooling around in his classes.

After a day of orientation and getting his flying gear issued, Mark was told he would learn to fly in what was to be the last bi-winged airplanes to be used in flight training by the Air Corps. The plane had two open cockpits, one behind the other. The instructor sat in the front seat, and the student in the rear. Instructors and students wore leather helmets, goggles, jackets, and gloves. It was one of the few airplanes left in which the pilot could fly and still feel the wind in his face.

To start the airplane's engine, someone had to stand on the lower wing near the front cockpit and turn a hand crank, causing a heavy flywheel to start spinning. After he got it spinning as fast as he could, the pilot would yell "Clear!" as a warning to anyone who might be near the propeller. The person doing the cranking would then pull a handle that engaged the flywheel to the engine, thereby making the propeller turn. The pilot then turned the switch on, and jockeyed the throttle to help the engine catch, and keep running. The person who had done the cranking jumped down off the wing and got out of the way.

The Mississippi Institute of Aeronautics, or MIA as it was called, was a delightful place, and Mark felt very lucky to be there. It had been a civilian flying school in peacetime, and some of the instructors, including Mr. Baxter, were kept on when the military leased it for primary pilot training. The one thing that bothered Mark was the school's initials, the same as Missing in Action.

Mr. Baxter taught Mark how to do take-offs and landings, power-on and power-off stalls, spins, slow rolls, loops, and Cuban eights. They practiced their take-offs and landings at the main field at MIA, and also on a small grass pasture a few miles away, which was used as their auxiliary field.

One of the things he had to learn to do very precisely was to hold a given heading and altitude, and to be careful not to gain or lose any altitude in a turn.

The plane had no radios, and the only way to communicate between the instructor in the front seat and the student in the back was by using gosports. They consisted of a funnel which the instructor spoke into, and which, in turn, was connected to a long rubber tube. The tube ran through the plane to the back cockpit, where it branched into two tubes that connected to the ear-flaps of the student pilot's helmet, looking and acting much like a doctor's stethoscope. When the instructor spoke into the funnel, the student could hear him through the tubing, over the noise of the wind and the engine. However, the student could not talk back.

If the instructor wanted to be really mean, when his student goofed during a maneuver, he could permit the funnel to hang out a little into the slipstream. This would allow the wind to enter the funnel, travel through the rubber tubes, and ram painfully against the student's eardrums. Whatever mistake you may have made, after that experience, you were very sure never to do it again.

CHAPTER 2

(Jackson, Mississippi, 1943)

After two weeks at the Mississippi Institute of Aeronautics, they were granted their first open post to go into Jackson. The bus left for town right after their Saturday morning parade.

Mark decided to go to the USO Dance. The United Service Organization was a civilian group made up of mostly volunteers. Its mission was to provide entertainment and comfort for soldiers during their off duty time.

Rooms were provided at most airports, train stations and downtowns in large cities. Soldiers could go there, get a free cup of coffee and read a magazine to kill time. They also sponsored dances and other social events.

The evening dances at the Jackson USO turned out to be a very special event, even though the dance floor was a basketball court in the armory during the daytime.

The girls wore evening dresses and looked very lovely. They also wore a bit more makeup than the northern girls he had grown up with and it seemed to bring more life and beauty to their lips and cheeks.

Some of their mothers sat in the bleachers, watching as the cadets danced with their daughters.

The music consisted mostly of Glenn Miller, Artie Shaw and Tommy Dorsey swing numbers provided by one of the mothers playing a 78 rpm record player, which sat on a table at one end of the room and was amplified by the PA system. Cadets who weren't dancing stood around the edge of the dance floor, trying to summon up enough nerve to ask a girl to dance, or to cut in on a couple already dancing.

Mark watched the dancers for a while, awed by the agility and gracefulness of some of them.

One girl in particular caught his eye. She was breathtakingly beautiful, with soft brown hair that fell in tender curls to her shoulders and a thoughtful smile that made you want to smile back. But it was her deep green eyes that were especially captivating.

She was dancing with a tall, good-looking soldier who swung her around effortlessly to Artie Shaw's "Temptation." He swooped her backward until her head nearly touched the floor, and then lifted her back up into his arms. Unfortunately, she had also caught the eye of many of the others, and was constantly being cut in on as she and her partner glided across the floor. Mark stood watching her for the longest time wondering if he could possibly muster up the courage to cut in on one of her dance partners.

His thoughts went back to the time in high school when recorded dance music was played over the PA system during lunch hour. The girls sat on one side of the gymnasium and the boys on the other. There were only three or four couples who ever danced and the rest of the students, who had finished their lunch, just sat on the bleachers and watched while waiting for the period to end.

One day Mark had decided he was going to ask a cute girl that he had had his eye on for some time to dance with him. It took all the willpower he could muster but he finally started his walk all the way across the gymnasium floor. There were only two couples out there dancing at the time, and he felt that everyone was watching him make his long, lonely trek. When he finally reached the girl and asked her for the dance, she said "No." His face became the shade of a ripe tomato as he turned to make the embarrassing trip back. He felt the eyes of the whole school witnessing his rejection. It was the most humiliating thing that had ever happened to him, and he never completely got over it.

However, that was then and this was now, and he was never going to win a fair damsel with a faint heart. So when the beautiful girl and her partner again neared his side of the room, he walked up and tapped him on the shoulder. The hapless fellow looked up in disbelief, and reluctantly released her to him.

His hand slid around the waistline of her fitted, red velvet dress and he sensed the smell of magnolias as he pressed her to him. He took a step backward then flung her out, made her do a spin and then drew her back into his arms again.

"Hi, I'm Mark Andrews," he said quickly.

"Hi, Mark, I'm Joanne Williamson." It seemed like the words had barely left her lips when he felt someone tapping his shoulder, and he hesitantly released her to her next partner.

The situation seemed hopeless. Mark did get to dance with her twice again briefly, but then resigned himself to either standing on the sidelines, or dancing with some of the other girls for the rest of the evening.

After a few more dances, the music stopped playing for some reason. While they were waiting for it to start up again, Mark started talking to Bob Eddy, one of the cadets he knew from the base. As they talked, Mark noticed that one of the matronly ladies on the other side of the dance floor was talking to a group of the girls, including Joanne. Bob was wondering why they had stopped the music, because he had been having so much fun dancing most of the dances. As they talked, Mark's eyes kept straying back across the room to Joanne as if she had some hypnotic spell over him. As he stood transfixed, staring at her, he found himself saying, half to Bob and half to himself: "See that girl over there? I'm going to marry her someday."

Mark could hardly believe what he had said. It was the first time he had ever considered marrying a girl, and this one, of course, was nothing more than a passing fantasy in a brief moment of his life. Bob turned to him and said, "Yes, she's beautiful all right; I've had my eye on her all night."

Finally the PA system sprung to life again with the announcement:

"We will now start the Grand March. Find yourself a partner and form a line at the center of the dance floor."

Well, Mark had no idea what a Grand March was, and really didn't care an awful lot. He had resigned himself to waiting it out until it was over before trying to dance again.

His gaze again drifted back across the room toward Joanne. She was turning away from the lady she was speaking with and started walking across the dance floor in his direction. Mark wondered where she was going and turned around to see if her mother might be in the bleachers behind him. But there wasn't anyone in the bleachers directly behind him, and yet Joanne kept coming. Much to Mark's utter amazement, she walked directly up to him and said, "Mark, I've been asked to lead the Grand March and wondered if you would be my partner?"

If there is such a thing as the magnetism of love, it must have been in full power at that moment to bring her over to him.

When he finally recovered from his shock, he had enough composure to say, "Who me?"

She smiled and said "Yes, you, Mark."

Still a bit stunned, he managed to reply, "Why, I'd be delighted."

He decided not to tell her that he had no idea what a Grand March was, because he didn't want to do anything at this point that might jeopardize his good fortune. He thought to himself, maybe I can fake it. I hope I don't make a fool of myself trying.

Joanne seemed to sense some of his anxiety, and took him by the hand and led him out to the middle of the dance floor. As if by magic, other couples hurried from different parts of the room and joined in behind them. Joanne turned to look at him and gave him a radiant smile that made the room light up. She also gave his hand a reassuring squeeze.

"Don't worry, Mark. Just watch me. It's easy."

When the music began, they started leading the procession down the center of the room toward the far end of the floor. As they reached the end, Joanne turned to the right, leading all the girls behind her. Mark turned to the left, leading all the guys behind him. When they completed marching all the way around the opposite sides of the room in time to the music, they met again at the front end of the dance floor. There they joined hands and held them high so as to make an arch for the rest of the couples to pass through, and they, in turn, added their arms to the arch for the following couples to go through. The last couple ended up going through the long arch made by all the other couples before them. After several more maneuvers and gyrations, the march ended, and the couples got to dance the rest of that dance with the same partner without being cut in on.

Mark was thrilled to be able to dance one complete number with Joanne without being interrupted. It not only gave him the chance to carry on some conversation with her, but best of all, it gave him the opportunity to get her phone number. When the Grand March ended, Joanne asked him to come with her for a few minutes. She had to go up into the stands to tell her mother something, and she wanted him to go along and meet her. Mrs. Williamson turned out to be a very pleasant, rosy-cheeked, blue-eyed Irish lady, a bit on the plump side, but with a very friendly smile. It turned out that she had sewn Joanne into her dress at the waist that evening. Joanne showed her where the seam was beginning to come apart due to the strenuous dancing. After exchanging a few more words with her mother, they returned to the dance floor, and once again Joanne was swept away from him. He managed to get one more short dance with her before he and some of the other cadets had to leave to catch their last bus to the base. As they walked down the street they could hear the sound of the Tommy Dorsey band playing "I'm Getting Sentimental Over You," fading behind them in the background.

For the next few days, all he could think of was her. If there was such a thing as falling in love, he guessed this was it.

But he had to get her off his mind long enough to learn to fly.

He had to learn to fly well enough to out fly a determined enemy— or he'd be dead.

CHAPTER 3

(Jackson, Mississippi)

One windy morning Mr. Baxter and Mark were shooting landings at their small, grass auxiliary field. They were having their usual one-way conversation with Mr. Baxter carrying on his continuous cranky dialog.

"Okay, there's our field down there. We'll use the one between the barn and the road. It's the one with the small tree next to the left fence.

"Set up your standard traffic pattern and enter your downwind leg at 45 degrees. There's a 15 mile an hour wind today and it's a slight crosswind, so you'll have to crab to correct for drift and be prepared to give more throttle on the approach."

As always, the conversation was one way, since Mark had no way to talk back.

He had approached his pattern altitude as he entered the downwind leg and was trying to judge where to start his turn onto his base leg. With the significant wind, he needed to start sooner than normal. As he looked over his left shoulder, he saw the fence appearing, and started his turn on to the base leg.

"You're a little close. Throttle back on your turn to final. Okay, watch your air speed. Prepare to chop power. Watch your drift. Give a little power to cross the fence. Okay, cut power for touchdown."

As his wheels touched the grassy field, he worked the brakes and rudder pedals, preparing to give it the power to take off for another go around, or come to a stop. There was a slight pause, and then Mr. Baxter said, "Pull over next to the fence by the tree."

As Mark pulled to a stop, he was surprised to see Mr. Baxter climbing out of the airplane without a word. Mark thought perhaps he had to get out to relieve himself. But then, he turned around and signaled for him to take it up.

This was a terrifying moment. It was the first time that Mark had been in an airplane alone with the engine running, and he had grown accustomed to having Mr. Baxter sitting in the front cockpit telling him exactly what to do. At the sight of his empty seat, and the complete silence, his grip on the stick tightened and he broke out into a cold sweat.

He revved up the engine and swung the plane around, taxied down to the south end of the field, and lined up into take-off position. He paused to carefully look around at the sky for other airplanes. When he felt that he was clear, he slowly and smoothly increased the power to full throttle, while easing in a bit of right rudder to counteract the torque of the prop. As the plane picked up speed, he continuously worked the rudder pedals back and forth so as to keep the plane headed on a straight course, and to keep it from ground looping: a notorious characteristic of the Stearman because of its wheels being so close together.

The plane gathered more and more speed. The tail began to lift and he slowly and smoothly eased the stick backward until the wheels left the ground. He was airborne!

He climbed up to the traffic pattern altitude of 800 feet, and he kept his eyes constantly moving over the basic instruments, confirming that his air speed and heading were constant. He looked out of the cockpit to make sure that he was clear of any other aircraft that might be flying in the area, and then turned left onto his downwind leg.

With every move he made, he could hear Mr. Baxter's voice in his mind saying, "Watch that altitude. Watch your air speed. Pick your landing spot. Watch it go under your wing. Start your turn onto your base leg. At the 45° point, pull your throttle back, now! Start your descent. Now start your turn onto final.

Watch your air speed. Watch your altitude. Start your flare as you go over the fence. Keep a steady back pressure. Keep the airplane at a 3-point altitude. That's the way. Steady now. Don't let it drift on you. A bit more right rudder…"

And then Mark felt the plane touch the ground, and start rolling on the grass. He had done it! He had soloed! But why was he so alone? Why weren't there bleachers full of people on both sides of the field cheering and yelling for him? This was too big a thrill not to share with the world.

He taxied up to Mr. Baxter, who looked up at him, then broke down and gave Mark a faint smile. It was a gesture that Mark took as a real compliment, for he rarely displayed any emotion whatsoever. His instructor climbed back into the plane, and they flew back to the main field.

Mark had never felt more excited and elated about anything in his entire life and wanted to tell everyone he saw about it. That night he was thrown into the shower fully clothed, as was the custom in the group whenever a cadet soloed for the first time. As soaked as he was, he would have been disappointed if they had not done it to him.

CHAPTER 4

(Jackson, Mississippi)

So far, Mark's training and maneuvers were all conducted in the local area. The day finally arrived when he would leave the vicinity and the comfort of the airfield to take his first solo, cross-country flight. It would not be a long flight, but it was like leaving home for the first time, with lots of anticipation and feelings of uncertainty. And there was always the possibility of getting lost.

He was to fly for about an hour and a half over several small Mississippi towns, Philadelphia, Kosciusko, and Yazoo City, and then fly home.

Mark worked hard planning his trip, drawing his course on maps, and marking off checkpoints for every ten minutes of flight. He also took extra care to fold the maps just right so that the start of the flight was on top, and so that they could be unfolded neatly as he progressed. He went over the course time and time again, picking out some prominent landmarks for additional checkpoints.

Finally, the day came for his trip. He walked out to his plane with his maps folded in their proper order and tucked into the knee pocket of his flight suit.

After taking off and climbing to 1,500 feet, he circled the field once, and turned the plane to his first heading. He looked at his watch and made a careful note of his starting time.

With the plane straight and level and on course, he reached down to his knee pocket for his maps, took them out, and started to unfold them.

Swoosh! All of the maps were suddenly sucked out of his hands, and out of the open cockpit. He watched in disbelief as he saw them spewing out into the vast expanse of the clear blue sky. Oh no! He was shocked! It was as if they were consumed by a giant vacuum cleaner.

Mark was dumbfounded. Nobody had ever warned him about the perils of the open cockpits. What was he going to do? If he went back and landed without completing his cross-country, he could be washed out.

He tried to remember his first leg. Let me see, he thought. The course direction was 32 degrees and the distance was 12 miles. At 104 miles per hour with a 5 mile an hour head wind it should take about 9 minutes. What was his first check point? Oh yeah, the small railroad bridge going from southwest to northeast.

Mark looked down at the landscape passing below, and saw what he remembered to be his first checkpoint coming up. It was the place where the railroad crossed a small river. He continued to fly over it, and noted the time. He then tried to remember the next checkpoint. It was the juncture of two roads near a small town. As he began to visualize it in his mind, he suddenly realized that he had worked so hard preparing his cross-country flight, that he had memorized the whole flight plan.

He completed the flight without any further problems, and never told his instructor that he had done it entirely without the aid of his maps.

When Mark landed and went back to the ready room, he sat down and went over the trip in his mind. Although nothing was said, he couldn't help but feel that the same experience of the vanishing maps must have happened to some, if not all, of the other pilots. In fact, their instructor Mr. Baxter undoubtedly knew it would happen, and wanted to see how his fledging pilots would handle the emergency.

* * * *

It was getting to be winter in Mississippi, and Mark thought there would be no problem keeping warm that far south.

However, once airborne, the temperature dropped considerably and the hundred miles an hour air stream blasted freezing air into the open cockpit of the Stearman. Even wearing his fleece-lined leather jacket, trousers, boots, gloves, and helmet, he was uncontrollably shivering.

One clear day, when it was much colder than usual, Mark had been flying for an hour and was miserable. All that he could think about was getting back on the ground and into the warm ready room, where he could stand next to a radiator and let some heat soak into his body.

When his time was finally up, he landed and taxied toward the hangar. As he approached the tie down area, he could see Mr. Baxter walking out of the ready room toward him. When Mark swung the plane around and pulled it to a stop in his parking slot, Mr. Baxter jumped up onto the wing.

"Take it up for another hour, Mark."

He couldn't believe his ears and was almost in tears, but he didn't dare complain. He took off again and flew around for the most miserable hour that he had ever spent.

* * * *

Primary flight training lasted two months. During that time, six students washed out, including some very athletic ones and seemingly well-coordinated ones. Somehow, Mark, who had never been a great athlete, did well.

The reasons for being washed out varied. Washing out meant that a cadet reverted to the rank of private and could never become a pilot. For some students, it was a lack of coordination, some for persistent air sickness, some for being accident prone, and some for being slow learners. A cadet could even be washed for having an attitude problem. Therefore, the cadets were always on their toes trying to do everything just right to make a good impression on their instructors.

****

There was a wonderful, unwritten code of honesty among the cadets, which gave them a good feeling of confidence and trust in one another. Mark knew that he could leave his wallet or any of his belongings on his bunk while he left to take a shower, or go eat dinner, and never worry about anything being stolen.

CHAPTER 5

(Jackson, Mississippi)

It rained for a few days during the week after he met Joanne, and the cadets were confined to the base for the weekend to make up their lost flying hours. Mark managed to call Joanne several times, and had, what he considered to be, rather disappointing conversations with her. It turned out that, for some unknown reason, she was not an easy person to talk with on the telephone. Nevertheless, he did manage to get a date with her for the following Saturday.

It wasn't until later on in the week that he learned the cadets would not be allowed to go to town Saturday until after they marched in a morning parade. Parading on Saturday morning was the last thing in the world that he wanted to do, and wished that he could figure some way to get out of it.

He overheard two cadets talking about going to the dentist on Dental Call Saturday morning. Apparently if you went on Dental Call, you wouldn't have to march in the parade because you would be taken into town by an ambulance to see the dentist. When the dentist was through with you, you were free to go on into town on open post.

Mark felt that if he thought about it hard enough, he did have a tooth that bothered him somewhat. So he decided to sign up for Dental Call, seeing this as the answer to his problem of how to get out of the parade, as well as to get into town early.

When Saturday morning arrived, he rode into Jackson in the back of an army ambulance with two other cadets, Jack Benson and Lou Douglas. They were taken to a civilian dentist who was under contract with the army.

When it was Mark's turn in the chair, the dentist probed around and finally hooked his pick on one spot on a back tooth which proved to be somewhat tender. Before he knew it, Mark had a large needle shooting Novocain in his gum. The dentist drilled on the tooth for about half an hour, and finally filled it.

Mark walked out of the dentist's office feeling punk, but felt that he had reaped his just reward for trying to pull something over on the Army Air Force.

At two o'clock, he went by Joanne's home to pick her up. She lived in a small apartment building in the middle-income section of town. Her mother, whom he remembered meeting at the USO dance, answered the door. She greeted him warmly and invited him in, saying that Joanne would be out in a moment, and then excused herself. Joanne immediately entered the room wearing an attractive white dress with a pleated skirt. She smiled and held out her hand to greet him. He was delighted to see her, and his pulse started beating a little faster. She said good-bye to her mother and they left to catch a bus to go downtown.

He wished more than anything that he was feeling better.

When they got into town, they walked around for a while, and then had a Coke in a café and talked. It turned out that they would only have a few hours together, because Joanne had a date for that evening.

She asked Mark if he had a girlfriend back home and he told her, no, that he didn't have a steady girlfriend. Surprisingly, Mark found that she did not seem to have a steady boyfriend either.

She told him that she enjoyed dancing, and had won second place in a Miss Jackson beauty contest. Mark thought that it was an outstanding achievement, but he could tell that she was a bit embarrassed by the fact that she hadn't won first. She was born in Memphis, but had lived in Jackson most of her life. She had just graduated from high school the previous summer, and was working as a secretary for an oil company.

Mark told her about his home, his two years of college, and enough of his army experiences to let her visualize how he got to Jackson.

All too soon it was time to take her home; and that was the end of their date, such as it was. It was nice, in that it did give them an opportunity to know one another better, but it left him a bit frustrated, and on top of that, his mouth was still numb from the Novocain, and he had a headache to boot. So in general, it had been an unfulfilling afternoon. He wondered if this was to be the end of the story about the beautiful girl with whom he had somehow fallen in love.

CHAPTER 6

(Greenville, Mississippi)

After finishing primary, Mark's class was sent to Greenville, Mississippi for two months of basic training. Here he would learn to fly a more powerful airplane, the BT-13. It had a glass canopy so he would no longer feel the wind in his face. And it made so much noise on take-off that it became known as the Vultee vibrator.

Mark noticed that whenever he got transferred to a new base, the food always seemed to taste better than it did at the last base, and the food at Greenville was the best yet. Everything in the chow line looked tempting and Mark piled up his plate. It turned out that he had taken much too much. When he went to the garbage can to scrape his plate clean, a lady lieutenant was standing there and said, "Mister, what's wrong with that food?"

Mark said, "Nothing, ma'am."

"Then take it back and eat it."

"Yes, ma'am."

Mark felt miserable finishing the food, but it taught him to never again take more than he could eat.

* * * *

The BT-13 was an easy airplane to fly and easy to roll.

Mark was flying with his instructor one day and rolled the airplane upside down for a bit of inverted flying. He didn't realize that he had a lot of change in the knee pocket of his flight suit and forgot to zip it closed. Since he was now upside down, all the coins fell out the pocket and landed on the plane's canopy. When

23

he rolled the plane back to the upright position, the coins all fell down through the floor openings to the bottom of the fuselage. The instructor, of course, heard the coins fall, and after a pause told Mark to unfasten his seat belt. He then started slowly rotating the plane upside down and had Mark work his way around the canopy so that his knees were always facing the ground. When the plane was completely inverted, flying upside down, the coins all fell back from the floor to the top of the clear plastic canopy that Mark was now kneeling on. He picked up the coins off the canopy and held on to them as the instructor righted the plane and Mark slid back into his seat. He put the coins back in his flight suit pocket and zipped it shut. It was another of the many lessons he was learning by experience.

There didn't seem to be any USO dances in Greenville and of course Mark missed dancing with Joanne. With the army transferring him every 2 months he had resigned himself to never seeing her again.

As usual, they had no idea where they were being transferred to next, until the day before they were to leave. Then there came a big surprise. Mark learned that they were being sent back to Jackson, Mississippi. They were going to be the first American cadets to use the main municipal airport there for their advanced flying training.

For the past year, it had been used to train Dutch cadets, who had escaped from Indonesia just before it was overrun by the Japanese. Apparently, all of them had now completed their training, and the empty base was being converted to an advanced flying base for American students.

Mark's immediate thoughts, of course, were of Joanne, and wondered if she would still remember him. After all, she had probably danced with several hundred other cadets since he had left. And she would also think that when he left Jackson to go to other flying schools for basic and advanced training, he would never be back.

Mark wondered if he still had her phone number. He may have thrown it away since he never expected to go back to Jackson to see her again. He searched frantically through his foot locker for it. With great relief, he found a little slip of paper with her number on it near in the bottom among other papers.

He hurried to a phone to call the minute he had a chance and her mother answered.

"Yes, Joanne is here. Just a minute, I'll call her."

She called Joanne for him, and the next thing he knew, he was talking to her again, and his heart started beating faster. "Yes, Mark, I do remember you. You say you're coming back to Jackson? What a pleasant surprise! Yes, I'm still going to the USO dances on Saturday night.

"Let's plan to meet there as soon as we can when you get back to Jackson?"

"That sounds like a good idea," Mark said, and when he hung up, he was walking on air. He could easily visualize her breathtaking beauty in his mind's eye; her long brown hair, her clear green eyes that could look right through him, her beautiful lips, and her fair, pale, unblemished complexion. He also remembered that her figure was beauty-contestant perfect and that she danced effortlessly.

When he arrived back in Jackson, it seemed like he had been gone for such a long time yet it had only been two months. But so much had happened to him in basic during those two months. He learned to fly a new airplane there, and had honed up his ability to fly under the hood using only his instruments.

Reaching advanced flying school was a big step in the life of a cadet. The instructors treated them with more respect than they had been given in primary or basic training. Perhaps it was because when they graduated here, they would become second lieutenants, or flight officers.

The rank of flight officer was a relatively new one, and was equivalent to the army's warrant officer. It was a rank offered to those who had the intelligence and technical skills required to be a pilot, but were evaluated as lacking the leadership qualities required to eventually become a commanding officer of a flying squadron.

The ratio of the two varied from class to class, but Mark had heard that it was something like 60 percent of the class would become officers (second lieutenants), and 40 percent would become flight officers. Needless to say, everyone was hoping to become a second lieutenant.

The airplanes that they would now fly in advanced training were the AT-6 Texans, made by North American Aviation. They were the first airplanes they would fly that had retractable landing gear. They were beautiful planes to look at and to fly, and were especially great for doing acrobatics.

One of the hardest maneuvers which they had to execute was the eight-point slow roll. In it, the plane is rolled 360°, but stopped briefly eight times on its way around. It is also necessary to use the opposite rudder from the direction the plane is rolling to keep the nose from falling while the plane is on its side—the left rudder for a right roll. As the pilot continues around until he is upside down, he has to press the stick forward to hold the nose up. Then as he continues around the other half of the roll, he has to ease in the right rudder to keep the nose from falling. While he is doing all of this, he has to stop the roll momentarily at eight different points, and then continue the roll again at each point. Finally, as he completes the roll, the pilot eases the controls back into their normal position, and is once more straight and level. If the pilot is really good, the nose will stay on a point on the horizon throughout the roll, and the plane will not have lost or gained any altitude.

This was the ultimate test of coordination, because the pilot had to fly the airplane right side up, upside down, and everywhere in between.

Mark had now learned how to take off; land; do level turns, slow rolls, snap rolls, loops, spins, immelmanns, and instrument flying under the hood; and how to navigate a cross-country flight. The only remaining obstacle was flying at night.

* * * *

Mark walked out to the flight line and found his airplane. He waited in line for his turn, then taxied into position for takeoff.

It was a very dark, moonless night and he felt very apprehensive at the thought of leaving the well-lit field and penetrating the dark void that faced him. As he took off and started his climb, he found that the sky was black and the ground was black, and that there was no visible horizon to tell him when he was straight and level. He had been warned that it was easy to experience vertigo under these conditions, and lose all sense of which way was up and which was down. He found himself frequently referring to his instruments, especially the artificial horizon, even though it was a clear night.

Around the airfield and the city, he could get some orientation help from the runway lights and the city lights. Once out in the country, however, he found it difficult to distinguish between the lights on the ground and the stars in the sky. He also knew that there were at least twenty other airplanes flying around the area which he had to be careful not to run into. One problem was that it was too dark to actually see the other airplane itself, all you could see of it was one of its lights. The red light would be on the left wing tip, the green light on its right wing tip, and the white light on its tail. Even if you did see a light, it was difficult to tell how close the other plane was.

Mark watched one red light moving across the front of his plane and then—swoosh!—it went whizzing by him, dangerously close.

The thought of his first night landing was quite frightening, but when he finally touched down, he was surprised to find that landing at night was not as hard as he expected it to be

He met Joanne the following Saturday night at the USO dance, and did not have much more luck dancing with her than he did the first time they met. She did, however, stop for a while, and came over to Mark, took him by the hand, and lead him up in the bleachers where her mother was sitting.

They sat there and talked for a few minutes. She admitted that when he had called her, she wasn't absolutely sure who he was. She thought she knew, and by arranging to meet him at the USO dance, it would give her a chance to look him over to see if she had been right.

They chatted a while, and then he asked her if he could have a date. It turned out that she already had a date for the next day and also for the following weekend, but she asked him to please call her, because she did want to have a date with him.

They returned to the dance floor, and once more he lost her to the onslaught of soldiers vying to dance with her.

Mark returned to the base that night with mixed emotions. He was pleased with the chance to see and talk to Joanne again, but frustrated that he didn't get to talk with her longer, nor have a date with her the following weekend.

The cadets finally reached the point in their schedule where tailors came in to measure them for their officers' uniforms. They had to pay for these themselves, but would be given a uniform allowance which would cover the basics. However, there were certain options which, if they wanted, they would have to pay for themselves. These included such things as a trench coat and a gabardine shirt to go with their trousers. This was a big thrill for Mark, because it made him feel that he was now getting close to graduation, and his officers' bars and wings were almost within reach.

CHAPTER 7

(Jackson, Mississippi)

As always, there was a certain amount of ground school Mark had to attend in addition to his flying training. This included classes in navigation, the theory of instrument flying, and meteorology.

Whenever the cadets entered a classroom, they always stood at attention in front of their seats until the instructor came in, walked up to his desk, and turned to them and said, "Seats!" Then they all sat down in unison.

They had one woman instructor who taught navigation. She was very cute, and pleasant enough, but strictly business. Mark was sure that he was not the only cadet in the room whose mind drifted away from navigation from time to time, fantasizing about being on a date with her.

The classes were not difficult, and things seemed to be progressing smoothly.

One of the cadets, Larry Lowell, with whom he had not been particularly good friends, surprised him one day when he came up to him and said, "I have a date Friday night and wondered if you would care to come along with us and my date's girlfriend? One of the girls has a car, and we will probably go dancing."

Mark was pleased to be asked, and since Joanne was tied up for the weekend and he had no other plans, he accepted. Larry went on to say, "The girls will pick us up outside the main gate at seven o'clock."

On Friday, when the time for their date arrived, Larry and Mark walked through the gate and up to the girls' car, which was parked by the curb, waiting for them.

As they approached the car, Mark saw who was sitting at the steering wheel. He was speechless. There was a pretty girl in the back seat whom he had never seen before, and in the front seat sat their lady navigation instructor.

Mark wondered which one was supposed to be his date, but Larry soon made it clear as he opened the door to the back seat and slid in. That left Mark to sit up front with the instructor.

"Mark, I'd like you to meet Kitty Williams," Larry said, "and I think you already know Betty Jenkins."

Mark turned and said hello to Kitty and then, somewhat sheepishly and cautiously, turned to his instructor, whom he had never called anything but "ma'am."

"Hello, Mark," she said.

He gulped and, somewhat hesitantly, managed to say, "Hello, —Betty."

It was just beginning to get dark as they started driving through town. Apparently, Kitty had forgotten something, and they were going to go back by her house to pick it up.

They kept driving until they were almost out of town. Eventually they turned down a side street. They continued past the place where the pavement ended and turned into a dirt road. The houses thinned out to a scattered few, and they finally stopped in front of one which was apparently Kitty's. The street was dark and there were no lights on in the house.

Kitty and Larry got out of the car and walked onto the porch. She fished around in her pocketbook for her key, found it, and opened the door. They then went in and closed the door behind them, then turned a light on in the living room.

Betty and Mark remained in the car, silent at first, but then they cautiously started some small talk, such as where they were from, and how they ended up in Jackson. He casually placed his arm along the back of her seat, and turned slightly to face her. He was beginning to feel a bit more at ease now, yet couldn't forget that this was his instructor. Monday morning he would be facing her in class under quite different circumstances.

They had grown quiet again, and Mark looked toward her and said, "Why don't you come closer?" He helped her make up her mind by drawing her to him with his arm that had found its way around her shoulder.

So far so good, he thought. At least she didn't reject me.

She sat there, nestled in his arm, very still. Mark didn't want to rush anything or make her angry in any way, so he got them talking a bit more about themselves. Then there was more silence. He slowly bent over toward her, they looked into each other's eyes, and he, ever so slowly, kissed her.

Her response was almost startling. Instead of objecting, she warmly melted in his arms and seemed to invite his advances.

He unbuttoned the top of her dress, pulled her brassiere down, exposing a breast, then bent down and kissed her. She gave a slight quiver and pulled him closer to her.

He stopped to look out at the dark house that still only had the one light coming from the living room window. He couldn't see any sign of Larry and Kitty.

Mark was a little reluctant to go much further with Betty, for fear they would come out and catch them in an awkward position. However, Betty was obviously warm and seemed to have no fear of the situation.

His hand slid down to her legs and rested on one of them. It felt nice as they continued kissing.

He suddenly realized that if they were to go any further, they should probably move into the back seat. The front of the car was a bit awkward with the steering wheel in the way.

When he suggested the back seat, she responded quickly by saying, "We can do it right here."

Mark could hardly believe his ears.

The next thing he knew, she swung one leg over him and straddled him as he sat on the passenger side of the front seat. He had never experienced this much aggression from a woman before.

He entered her, and they made almost violent love. She moaned and moaned and seemed to get every bit as much pleasure from it as he did.

They were both aware that the other couple would be coming out of the house at any time, so they quickly cleaned up and got dressed. Their timing was just about right, for Larry and Kitty appeared at the car door soon afterward.

"Sorry to keep you waiting," Larry said.

"That's okay," Mark said. "It gave Betty and me a chance to get better acquainted."

They went dancing for a while at a small nightclub. Betty was a good dancer and Mark enjoyed swing dancing with her to Benny Goodman's Careless Love, and especially his Stompin' at the Savoy.

At 1:00 a.m., the nightclub closed and the girls drove them back to the base. Mark kissed Betty goodnight, and couldn't help but wonder how they would feel and behave in her classroom come Monday.

The next day was Saturday, and since the weather had been good enough for the cadets to accomplish the required flying for the week, they had Saturday and Sunday free for open post.

CHAPTER 8

(Jackson, Mississippi)

Mark went to town with his friend, Warren Jackson. Warren was a "good ole' southern boy," rather tall and good-looking, and was also one of the few cadets who was married. However, he never spoke of his wife.

As with any healthy, young American male alone on the weekend, Warren was not averse to looking at a pretty girl. He had a charm about him that attracted them, and sometimes resulted in unexpected experiences.

Warren and Mark decided to stay in town that night and checked into the Heidelberg Hotel. After dropping their shaving kits off in their room, they started walking around town. Warren had written a letter and wanted to go by the post office to buy a stamp and mail it.

Mark followed him into the post office and waited near the long counter against the wall. He looked at the special delivery forms and postal information under the glass top as he waited.

A very nice-looking young lady in her early twenties was at the counter licking stamps and putting them on the pile of letters in front of her. After Warren finished mailing his letter, he walked back toward Mark, and paused momentarily by the lady and asked, "What are all those letters you're mailing?"

Why can't I ever think of an opening line like that, Mark wondered.

"I work in a doctor's office," she said, "and I'm mailing out the monthly bills for him."

"Why don't you come and have a Coke with us?" Warren asked.

She smiled a beautiful smile, glanced at Warren and then at Mark, and then cautiously said, "I don't know—."

Well, Mark could see that this was the signal to Warren that the fish had taken a small nibble of the bait, and now was the time to turn on all his charm and reel her in.

A few more words of small talk, and the next thing he knew the three of them were walking down the street toward the main drag, talking up a storm. Her name was Laura Jane, she was married to a guy in the navy who had been overseas for a year, and she had hardly been out of the house except to go to work at the doctor's office.

They went to the little Greek restaurant and soda fountain on Capitol Street, sat in a booth, and asked her if she wanted anything to eat. She declined, explaining that she was living with her mother while her husband was gone, and that she was expected home for dinner. So they just ordered three Cokes.

As usual, Mark was a slow starter, but once the conversation got going, he was at ease. Warren was doing most of the talking, but it turned out that he already had plans for later on that evening, so he was not pushing for her to come back.

Mark suggested that she come back when she had finished supper at home, and go to a movie with him. He said that he would wait for her in front of their hotel.

They looked up as two other couples came into the restaurant and sat in the booth directly across the aisle from them. Mark recognized the two cadets from the base, but was startled to see who one of their dates was. She was none other than his passionate lover from the night before—their navigation instructor: Miss Betty Jenkins.

Mark suddenly felt a bit awkward and found his words not flowing as smoothly as they had before. But even though he was somewhat distracted, he heard their table companion saying, "Well, I guess it would be all right."

Mark suddenly came back to his senses, and realized that he had just gotten a date with Laura Jane that evening.

After fifteen more minutes of small talk, they finished their Cokes, and stood up to leave. The foursome in the other booth looked up at them, said "Hello," and for the first time Betty's eyes met his. She smiled, and they paused briefly at the table. Mark felt for some reason that he should introduce their instructor to Laura Jane.

Much to his surprise, Betty shook his hand and said it was nice to see him again. Mark suddenly realized why she was shaking it, as he felt a small scrap of paper in her palm passing in to his. Thank goodness he had the presence of mind to accept the note without letting anyone see it. He palmed it discreetly, and slipped it into his pocket as they walked out of the restaurant.

When they got outside, Laura Jane said that she had to leave, and confirmed to Mark that she would meet him in front of the Heidelberg Hotel at seven o'clock.

When she turned and walked away, he waved good-bye and slowly pulled Betty's note from his pocket. He unfolded the small piece of paper and read its message: Call me. 752-9301.

Mark could not believe what was happening. He had never been in such a situation in his life. What should he do?

He wandered around town for about an hour, and then returned to his room at the hotel. He sat down at the desk and tried calling the number on the slip of paper. He was a bit surprised when Betty answered, because he was not sure if she had had time to get home.

Mark asked her if she was free to talk, but she answered that she was not. Mark gave her the name of his hotel and the room number, and added, "Call me if you get a chance."

At ten minutes before seven, Mark went down to stand in front of his hotel, and waited for Laura Jane to arrive. It was a nice night, and, as was the case everywhere now, practically all the men who passed by were in uniform. Some were with dates, but most were without, wandering around aimlessly, looking for something to do, and trying to kill time.

He was beginning to wonder if he had been stood up when he saw Laura Jane approaching in the distance. He walked down the street to meet her, and they greeted each other with big smiles.

Mark was not quite sure if he should offer her his arm because he didn't know if she would be worried about being seen with him. This was her home town, after all, and she was married. This was also the first time that he had ever been out with a married woman, and was not quite sure how to act.

They arrived at the movie theatre, where a musical was playing starring Alice Faye and Don Ameche. He bought their tickets, and they went in, choosing two seats near the back.

After watching the movie for a while, Mark reached for Laura Jane's hand and held it warmly in his own. He was pleased that she made no effort to pull it away. As they continued watching the movie, his hand made love to her hand—rubbing her fingers, stroking down in between them, rubbing her warm palm. She accepted his flirtation by responding with a caressing squeeze from time to time.

When the movie ended, he asked her if she would come to his room for a while. She asked him if he thought it would be all right. He responded, "Sure, there won't be any problem."

They walked to the hotel, through the lobby, and up to his room. He was beginning to feel wild with anticipation. But in the back of his mind lurked the fear that Warren might be in there with his date.

As he opened the door, he was relieved to find the room empty. He walked up behind Laura Jane, who had stopped to look at herself in the mirror. Slipping his arms around her waist, he kissed her on the back of the neck.

She threw her head back as he continued kissing her. His hands slid up to her breasts, and she put her hands over his hands as he caressed them. At first, he thought that she was doing this to stop him, but instead she held them more firmly against her.

While they both stood there looking into the mirror, he slowly unbuttoned her blouse. He slid one hand inside of her blouse and cupped her brassiere. Then, as they watched, he slid his hand down under her brassiere strap and onto the softness of her bare breast.

She seemed to give a slight shudder, and then turned to him so that they could kiss each other fully on the lips. Their kiss was both passionate and tender. Locked in their embrace, they tumbled onto the bed together.

He decided that he had better begin undressing and did so as she removed her dress, which was already halfway off, and then her under things. It was warm in the room, so rather than pull the bed covers back, they reclined on top of the smooth sheets naked.

She reacted warmly and gave a soft moan and squirmed a bit as she spread her legs slightly. As their movements became more and more intense, they became carried away with passion. Mark had never seen such an attractive girl who was so responsive to his advances and lovemaking. As they reached their climax, the phone rang!

Damn it! he thought. Of all times for the phone to ring! He reluctantly stopped and thought a moment, trying to decide whether to get up and answer it or ignore it. It was probably Warren wanting to know if the coast was clear for him to come up to the room. Mark didn't want him walking in on them, so he went over to the desk, sat down on the chair, picked up the phone, and said, "Hello."

The voice on the other end said, "Hello," and paused. It definitely was not Warren's voice! It was a very feminine voice. It was Betty Jenkins, his navigation instructor! He had completely forgotten about their phone conversation earlier.

"How are you?" he asked her.

"Fine," she said. "Are you tied up?"

"Yes."

"Are you going to be tied up all evening?" she asked.

"No," he said. "How about calling me back at about half past ten?"

"Maybe," she replied.

They said good-bye, and he hung up. Laura Jane, meanwhile, had been lying quietly on the bed, looking at the ceiling and taking in the conversation.

"That was another girl, wasn't it?" she said.

"Yes."

"You're going to see her after me, aren't you?"

"No," he said. "We'll just talk on the phone. That's all."

She was pouting a bit, but after he went back to her and kissed and caressed her, they were soon making love again, even more passionately than before. After he reached his climax, they lay close to each other, and he continued to fondle her, and kiss her tenderly. Soon he was back on top of her, making love again, and she seemed to be enjoying every moment of it.

Suddenly their reverie was shattered by a knock on the door. Mark couldn't believe this was happening to him. He rolled over onto his elbow and looked at the door, wondering if it was Warren.

"Who is it?" he called out.

The frightening response came back loud and clear: "Open up! This is the hotel detective!"

Mark jumped out of bed, grabbed his shirt and trousers, and put them on as he stumbled toward the door, which was at the end of a short corridor that passed by the bathroom.

He opened the door a bit and looked out. Yes, there was the hotel detective standing in the hallway, along with an MP.

"What's the problem?" he asked.

"Do you have a woman in your room?" the detective inquired.

Mark answered, "Yes. Is there anything wrong with that?"

"You're not registered as man and wife," he replied, "that's what's wrong with it!" As he spoke, he pushed the door open and elbowed his way in.

Mark was petrified. He had just left Laura Jane in bed, completely naked, and felt that she wouldn't have had anywhere near enough time to get dressed by now. As they all entered the room, however, there she stood, fully dressed in front of the mirror, putting on her lipstick. The detective looked at her and rudely asked, "What's your name?"

She hesitated to answer, and Mark sprung to her defense and said, "You have no right to question her like that. She is a lady who was just up here visiting me."

"Oh, yeah?" he said. "Well, it's either I question her or the judge questions her downtown!"

That remark cooled Mark down rather quickly. He decided that caution might be the better part of valor at this point, and stood listening as the detective continued to question her, asking where she lived, how long she had lived there, and so on. Mark felt helpless and ashamed for her, and a bit worried for himself. There were only a few weeks left until his graduation from flying school, and a brush with the law could change all that he had been working so hard for all this time.

Finally, the detective turned to him and said, "You had better get her home right away, and I better never catch her here again."

"Yes, sir," Mark said.

When the detective and the MP left, they quickly finished dressing, and Mark said "I'm so sorry things turned out this way." Strangely, as she finished touching up her makeup, she seemed to be much calmer about the whole incident than he was. Mark was relieved that she didn't show any ill feelings toward him.

As they walked down through the lobby, he noticed Warren sitting across the lobby in one of the stuffed chairs. He excused himself from Laura Jane for a moment and went over to talk with him.

Warren said that he had overheard the discussion in the room with the house detective as he was standing in the hallway outside, and he had decided to go back down to the lobby and wait until Mark and Laura Jane came down. Mark explained to Warren what had happened, and went on to say that he might get a call from Betty Jenkins later on.

"Whatever happens," he said, "please don't let her come up into the room!"

Warren said that he understood; and with that, Mark left him and returned to Laura Jane. He walked with her out to the sidewalk, where he hailed a cab and took her home. He again apologized for the embarrassing situation, and kissed her good night. He took the cab back to the hotel, but then decided to walk down to the Pro Station before going back up to his room, just to be safe. (A Pro Station was a place run by the military in cities near military bases, where soldiers could go after having sex for prophylactic treatment. It was designed to prevent the contraction of venereal disease).

Upon returning to the hotel and walking into the lobby, he noticed two MPs back at the registration desk talking to the night clerk. The elevators were located near the desk, and as he started to enter one of them, an MP (the one who had accompanied the hotel detective earlier) turned toward him and said, "Your buddy's in trouble."

Mark looked at him, puzzled. "He is? Where is he?" he asked.

"He's upstairs. He'll tell you all about it when you see him."

Now what's this all about? Mark wondered, as he rode up to their floor.

He tried to think. Perhaps it was some girl that Warren had picked up while he was taking Laura Jane home. Wow! That was one fast, smooth southern boy when it came to picking up women.

The elevator reached his floor, the doors opened, and he walked down the hall toward their room.

Maybe, he speculated, Warren had called up the girl he had had a date with earlier and asked her up to his room.

Mark knocked on the door, and Warren opened it. He was bare-chested, wearing only his trousers.

"What's the problem?" Mark asked.

"How did you hear about it?"

"The MP mentioned it to me as I was getting on the elevator."

Warren looked at him sheepishly, shook his head, and with a slight grimace said, "Betty Jenkins got arrested."

"What? Betty Jenkins got arrested!" Mark couldn't believe his ears. He was in panic. He could see his career going up in smoke.

"How in the world did that happen?" he asked, staring open-mouthed at Warren.

"Well," he replied, "after I saw you down in the lobby, I came up to the room, took off my shirt, and was sitting at the desk writing a letter. About fifteen minutes later, there was a knock on the door, and when I answered it, lo and behold, who was standing there? None other than Betty."

"But surely you didn't let her in!" Mark said. "I told you under no circumstances to let her in! That was the last thing I told you down in the lobby before I left—not to let her in!"

"I let her in."

"Egad! How could you do that?"

"I don't know," Warren replied. "I guess I didn't have the nerve to turn her away. Perhaps it's my southern upbringing. But anyhow, I told her that I expected you back shortly, and she came in and sat on the bed while I continued writing my letter."

"So, the two of you did nothing together?" he asked skeptically.

"No, nothing at all. I was just sitting there writing my letter, and after a few minutes, there's a knock on the door. I thought it was you returning, but it turned out to be the house detective and an MP. They came in, asked her a few questions, and the next thing I knew, they were taking her down to the police station."

Mark went pale. Betty Jenkins, their navigation instructor, in the police station! "God!" he exclaimed. "There goes my career!"

He paced back and forth, wondering what to do. "I can't believe it! I can't believe it! What can I do? What should I do?"

He decided he had better call the police station, and perhaps go down to see what he could do for her, if anything. Frantically he searched for the telephone book and found it in one of the desk drawers. He found the number for the police station, and had the switchboard operator dial it for him.

After a few rings, the desk sergeant answered. Mark had never talked to a desk sergeant before. In fact, he had only talked to about two policemen in his life, and was not quite sure what to say.

"I'm inquiring about a Miss Jenkins, who I understand is being held there at your station," he began.

"Just a minute," the desk sergeant said. "Oh, yes. Miss Jenkins was brought in and released a little while ago."

Mark tried to think of what to say next, but couldn't think of how to phrase any of the many questions running through his mind: What is she charged with? Will she have to go to jail? If so, when and for how long? So he ended up just saying "Thank you," and hung up.

But come Monday morning he would have to face the situation head on, because he would be in her second period class again. How in the world was he possibly going to face her?

The next day, Sunday, dragged on endlessly. He did manage to get Joanne on the phone in the afternoon, and she agreed to go out with him the following Saturday.

Funny, he thought. My relationship with Joanne doesn't appear to be going anywhere. We've never had a real date. Our total time dancing together has been perhaps less than a half an hour. We have only kissed a few times and probably spent more time talking on the phone than we have face-to-face. Yet, the thought of her always keeps drifting back to me. Somehow—and I'm not sure how it will come about—but somehow I feel she is the girl I'm going to marry, and I'm not going to be completely sexually aggressive with her. I guess I'm telling myself that she is the one girl I want to save until after our wedding.

The dreaded Monday finally arrived. Mark saw no sign of Miss Jenkins on the way to class, and wondered if she was in school or had to go back to jail. Come second period, he stood at attention looking straight ahead at the blackboard when, to his relief, Miss Jenkins walked in and barked, "Seats!" He took his seat and tried to look anywhere in the room except at her. She went right into her lecture, and as the class progressed, he carefully looked her way several times. She never gave a sign of recognition, or any indication that this day was different from the rest of them. He sensed that the charges against her had been dropped, and she was prepared to go on with her life without him.

CHAPTER 9

(Jackson, Mississippi)

The next day, after the cadets had finished marching to the flight line and entered the ready room, they were greeted with some shocking news. The Air Corps had decided that it was training too many pilots and would be reducing the size of the graduating class by forty percent. That meant that four out of every ten of them would not graduate. Instead of becoming pilots and officers in three more weeks, they would be reverted to privates in the army.

Mark was petrified. The big question that immediately came to his mind was how the selection was going to be made. Who was going to be eliminated and how?

The answer started to become apparent in the next few days.

Each day they marched from their barracks down to the ready room on the flight line. Here they would sit and wait, passing the time when they weren't flying by reading one of the flight manuals or a magazine.

The door to the instructor's office was located at one end of the long room, and each time that door opened, they all looked up as an instructor entered the room, pointed his finger at a cadet, and indicated that he was to accompany him for a check ride. It soon became apparent that this was the signal of doom, and they knew immediately that it meant the cadet would not pass his check ride, and would be washed out.

The next three weeks were hell.

To make matters worse, the new officers' uniforms, which they had been measured for a few weeks earlier, were beginning to arrive. Each man looked at his uniform hanging on his rack in the barracks and wondered if he would ever get to wear it.

Mark survived the first wave of elimination rides.

CHAPTER 10

(Jackson, Mississippi)

Saturday finally arrived for his date with Joanne. He went to her house by street car to pick her up. They then rode the street car back to the base to see a movie. As usual, there was a long line waiting for tickets, and when they finally got into the theatre, it was packed. The movie was something about a family named the Foys and was ok, but the best thing about it was that it gave him a chance to hold hands with Joanne, and it made him feel very close to her.

After the movie, they walked around the base, looking for a place where they could sit and talk and, Mark hoped, perhaps pet a bit. The big problem was that as a cadet, he was neither fish nor fowl. Since he was not an officer, he could not use the officers' club, and since he was not a private, he could not use the enlisted men's club, and since he was not a sergeant, he could not use the NCO club. There was a small, one-room building, however, which had been designated as the cadet lounge. Mark headed for it.

After walking for about twenty minutes, he and Joanne reached the lounge and wandered in. There were very few cadets stationed at the base who were married, and it seemed that they were using the lounge to visit with their wives. So even in the cadet lounge, they could not find a place to sit, and even if they could, they would feel that they were intruding in on the few rare moments that these couples had to visit with each other.

So they went back out and started walking around again, hoping to find some dark place where they could have a bit of privacy. They finally found a relatively dark, quiet street, and Mark turned and took her in his arms and kissed her. She submitted to the kissing, but did not respond with any warm feelings to speak of, and it left him feeling somewhat empty.

Disappointed at not finding a more comfortable, private place, they finally walked back out the gate and caught a bus, and Mark took Joanne home.

When they entered the front door of her apartment house, Mark noticed that there was a staircase in the hallway leading to the upstairs apartment. He persuaded Joanne to sit on the steps with him for a while.

She agreed, but it soon became apparent that she mainly wanted to talk, and he mainly wanted to pet. She wanted to know about his girlfriend back home, but he wanted to kiss her some more. She wanted to know what he had done before entering the service, but he wanted to caress her breasts. She pushed his hand away, though not too firmly and not until he had had a very pleasant feel.

She finally said that she had to go in, but paused long enough to ask him if he would please call her again. He was surprised that she still seemed to want to see him again when their dates had all been so mundane, but he assured that he would call her during the coming week. She gave him a short goodnight kiss, and then he ran to catch the last bus back to the base.

As if things were not bad enough during their final weeks of training, to add to their misery, it began to rain. Each day of rain meant missing a day of flying training, and that meant that they would have to make up for it by flying on the weekends. In other words, there went their open post. Mark was really bothered because he knew that he was definitely falling in love with Joanne, and his remaining available time to see her was gradually dwindling down to zero.

He called her and told her about the situation, explaining that he could not get any more time off the base to be with her. Much to his surprise, she said that she was willing to take the bus out to see him on the base.

50

True to her word, she did take the bus to the base once during each of the remaining weekends.

Mark would meet her at the gate, and take her to the movie. Afterward, they would walk around until they found a lawn or the stairs of some darkened building, where they did a bit of necking. As unexciting as it seemed to be, somehow the ties between them grew stronger and stronger.

Mark survived the elimination ride selections, and it looked as though he was going to make it to graduation to get his wings. On his last day of flying, his instructor told him that he still needed two hours of flying time to complete his total requirements, and instructed him to take up a plane and just fly around for a couple hours. This was to be his last flight before graduation. He felt that all the pressures he had previously been subjected to while under the scrutiny of an instructor were gone. For the first time, he could relax and do anything with the airplane he wanted to. One of the things that they had been constantly admonished not to do all through their flight training, was not to fly too close to a cloud, and never to fly into one because you never knew if another airplane might be coming through it from the other side.

They never did actually fly in bad weather, but they did practice instrument flying "under the hood," with their instructors sitting in the other seat acting as a lookout for them. This would help them fly home safely if they were ever caught out in a storm.

Well, here he was on his last flight as a cadet, flying in the sky practically by himself, since most of the pilots had completed their required hours by that time.

It was a beautiful day, and yes, there was one gorgeous, fluffy cloud sitting out there all by itself. He climbed his way up to it and flew around it once to satisfy himself that there were no other airplanes in the vicinity. He then decided he was going to fly straight through it.

He wanted to be sure everything was perfect, so he caged and uncaged the artificial horizon. It was an instrument that had a bad tendency to drift after flying for a while, and give false indications of one wing being low when you were actually flying straight and level. So it had to be reset often. Mark flew away from the cloud for a few minutes, so as to gain some distance between him and it. He then turned toward it and lined up so as to fly right through its center. He cross-checked his instruments, making sure that he held his directional gyro on course and his wings level as he approached it. Just to make sure, he caged and uncaged his artificial horizon one more time before entering the cloud.

As he started to enter it, he concentrated on his instruments. Out of the corner of his eye he could see himself penetrating the wispiness of the cloud, and then suddenly become completely immersed in its eerie silence, and complete whiteness. Mark concentrated on his instruments, for now all references to the ground were gone. He maintained his directional gyro heading, his altitude, and his steady airspeed. The little airplane on the attitude gyro assured him that he was flying straight and level.

This was exciting! This was the most daring thing that he had ever done! He was exhilarated! Everything was perfect. He flew so carefully and accurately that the instruments seemed to be glued in their positions.

Then the wispiness started returning, suggesting that he was starting to emerge on the other side of the cloud. As he emerged, he was completely startled to find himself flying straight ahead, but in a fairly steep bank!

How could that be? His artificial horizon showed that he was flying straight and level. He quickly reached down to the instrument and checked the caging knob and found that the last time he had reset it, he apparently did not turn the knob back far enough to release it , and it was still caged. It would have indicated that he was flying straight and level no matter what attitude he was in. Luckily for him, he had flown through a relatively small cloud, rather than the extensive kind such as you find in a weather front. It could have been disastrous. Mark was beginning to think that in spite of all the great instructions they were getting, there were some things that a pilot learns by himself, and those were the things that left the most lasting impressions.

CHAPTER 11

(Jackson, Mississippi)

Now that the flying was done, it was all over but the shouting. The only three unknowns lurking in the immediate future were: Was he going to graduate as a second lieutenant or as a flight officer? Would he be made a fighter pilot or a bomber pilot? And where would he be sent to from here?

The pilots were marching from the flight line back to the barracks at the end of the day, singing, "I've been working on the railroad," in cadence, when one of the cadets ran down the road toward their formation, signaling for their leader to stop.

"Our orders are posted!" he yelled.

Everyone knew what that meant. They all broke ranks and ran full speed to the barracks area to search the new set of orders that had just been posted. They crowded around the large bulletin board, each one trying to elbow his way up to the front to eagerly search for his own name. What they read there resulted in the yelling out of "Wahoo!" from some, and blank looks of disappointment from others. Mark was finally able to get close enough to look at the list.

He spotted his name, and read it over and over again, trying to reassure himself that it was true. Seemingly bigger than life were his name, rank, and serial number, along with the name of his next duty station: Mark W. Andrews, 2nd Lieutenant, United States Army Air Force, Serial No. 8295632, Selma, Alabama.

It was Friday, and the graduation ceremony wouldn't be until Sunday. Needless to say, a lot of them wanted to go out and celebrate, and lost no time arranging an impromptu party to be held at "The Roof," of the Heidelberg Hotel.

Mark rushed to the phone to call Joanne. Luckily she was home, and he was able to give her the good news. She was delighted to hear that he achieved the goals he had worked so hard for all these months. "Congratulations Mark. You certainly deserve it," she said.

He told her about the party they were planning that evening and asked her if she would go with him. She said she would be delighted to go.

When they arrived at the Heidelberg Hotel and took the elevator to "The Roof" night club, they found it in full swing and jumping in a very nice sort of way. The band was playing Glenn Miller's "String of Pearls," and the large dance floor was almost filled.

Mark felt very proud as he introduced Joanne to his group. She looked absolutely stunning in her green taffeta dress, which dramatically emphasized her soft emerald eyes.

The group had pushed several tables together, and soon all were talking excitedly about the good news they had gotten that day, and where they were being reassigned to.

Mississippi was a dry state. It meant that people couldn't walk into a store and buy a bottle of liquor, nor could they order alcoholic drinks at a night club such as the one that they were in. They were allowed to bring a bottle of liquor with them, provided that they kept it in a paper bag and set it on the floor, not on the table. Mark drank very little and did not bring a bottle with him, so he and Joanne ordered Cokes. Someone in the group, however, did bring a bottle of whiskey, and it was soon being passed around to share with the rest of them. Mark poured a bit into their Cokes, and then passed it along.

When the band started playing "In the Mood," Mark and Joanne lost no time in joining the crowd on the dance floor. They stayed and danced the next number, "Begin the Beguine," and then went back to join the group at the table.

The bottle that had been passed around had gone dry by now, and Mark thought that it would be nice if he volunteered to go buy another one for the group. He had never bought a bottle in Mississippi before, but understood that there were several places in town where you could get one. One that he had heard the guys talking about in the barracks was the small hotel next to the Heidelberg. There you could buy a bottle in the lobby. So Mark decided to give it a try, and asked Joanne to go with him.

They took the elevator down to the lobby, and Mark suggested that she wait in one of the easy chairs for him while he went next door.

When he walked into the small hotel, he spotted a colored elevator man sitting on a stool by the elevator at the left side of the room. Mark approached him and asked "Where can I by a bottle of whiskey?" The man grinned a bit and pointed toward the desk on the other side of the lobby. Mark could see the reception desk with a dignified, white-haired lady standing behind it, and there were two doors to the right of it. As Mark approached the desk, she looked up and asked what she could do for him.

"I'd like to buy a bottle," he said, a bit awkwardly.

She turned pale, then red. "What?"

Mark was taken aback a bit by her reaction, but had heard any number of cadets say that they had bought bottles there. So he stood his ground, and repeated his request. "I'd like to buy a bottle of whiskey."

She immediately became very indignant and started banging the bell on the desk, summoning the house detective. "What do you think I am?" she exclaimed. "How dare you!"

The next thing he knew, he was surrounded by the hotel detective and two MPs.

Oh no, he thought, here I go again—and only two days before my graduation.

The lady told the detective about the grave insult that Mark had inflicted upon her; she was obviously the flower of southern gentry.

The detective turned to Mark, "I believe you owe this lady an apology."

Mark lost no time in apologizing, "I'm so sorry if I offended you, but I was told that I could buy a bottle here." Unfortunately, it did not calm the lady down in the least bit, and the next thing Mark knew, he was being escorted out of the lobby by the two MPs.

He was arrested!

Again, he could visualize his entire career going up in smoke. And to make matters worse, his girlfriend was waiting for him in the lobby next door. How would he get word to her that he was being arrested?

When they got to the sidewalk in front of the small hotel, the two MPs turned to him, and one of them said, much to his surprise, "Stay away from this place!"

It took a few seconds for Mark to realize they were releasing him. He thanked them and returned to the lobby of the Heidelberg, where he picked up Joanne, and they went back up to join their group, empty-handed.

When he related the incident at the table, one of the cadets, who had bought liquor there before, laughed and said "You should have gone into the men's room—the door just to the right of the desk—and bought the liquor from the shoeshine boy!"

Needless to say, Mark didn't volunteer to go back. One of the other cadets did, and successfully returned with a bottle fifteen minutes later.

After the party, he walked Joanne home, and she seemed somewhat warmer than she had been in the past. They sat on the steps in the hall of her apartment, as they had done before. They both knew that his time in Jackson was drawing to a close. They also knew that they both felt something much more powerful than a casual relationship that would soon be forgotten.

They began to neck pretty heavily, and she allowed him more liberties than she had in the past. Mark held himself in check, however, and in spite of the passion that was welling within him, only allowed himself to go so far.

He realized he was in love with her.

He had never said the words to any other girl before, because he held them to be sacred, and not to be used lightly, but after a long, labored pause, he said them to Joanne.

"I love you."

That night, on his way back to the base, Mark was walking on air.

The graduation ceremony was held on a Sunday afternoon. Joanne attended, and pinned his wings above the left breast pocket of his jacket, and his gold bars onto his shoulders. Mark had never felt more proud. However, Joanne had to leave almost immediately because of a previous engagement with her family.

As the new officers left the auditorium, they were met by a battery of soldiers who wanted to be the first to salute them. Traditionally, a new officer gave a dollar to the first person who saluted him, and some of the more enterprising men had fists full of dollars.

They were given a five-day leave upon graduating. Most of them went home to spend it with their parents, including Mark.

CHAPTER 12

(Wilmington, Delaware; Selma, Alabama)

Mark had a nice visit with his mother and Uncle Max and Aunt Betty, but all of his buddies were in the service and away somewhere on duty. He did have two dates with Shirley, his former girlfriend. She had been married and divorced since he had last seen her.

His leave was soon over, and he got on a train taking him from Wilmington back south to Selma, Alabama. It was the first time that he was being assigned to a new station as an officer, and did not have to travel by troop train. It gave him a new sense of freedom and responsibility.

The train was fairly crowded, but he was able to find a seat next to an army sergeant, and stowed his B-4 bag in the rack above them.

How simple life in the service becomes, he thought. Here I am with everything I own in one bag on the shelf above me.

He tried to do some reading, but the sergeant was a talkative sort, so he was not having much success. The train was a regular civilian train, not a troop train, so it made many stops at stations along the way, taking on and letting off passengers.

Time dragged, and at one stop the sergeant said, "Come on, Lieutenant, let's get off here a few minutes and stretch, and I'll buy you a cup of coffee."

Mark hesitated, and asked "I wonder if that would be such a good idea?" He felt uncomfortable about there being enough time.

But the sergeant was persuasive, and the next thing he knew, they were drinking coffee together at the counter inside the station. He was nervous as a cat and, sure enough, when they finally returned to the platform, the only sign of their train was a thin wisp of smoke disappearing down the tracks and over the horizon.

Mark could have killed the sergeant. Everything I own is on that train! he thought. What am I going to do?

A conductor had been standing a short distance up the platform from them. Observing their plight, he came over to them and said, "I see you missed your train. Perhaps I can help you. Your train is actually in two sections. The second section is a navy troop train, and will be coming along in a few minutes. I can put you aboard it when it arrives."

In a few minutes, the next section pulled in, and they found themselves climbing aboard a strange type of troop train. It consisted of gray boxcars. Each one was fitted with two levels of bunks around the inside walls and a stove in the middle. There were no windows, so the big doors had been slid open to provide ventilation and a view of the passing countryside.

They felt a little awkward standing next to the unlit stove with about a dozen sailors sitting around on their bunks looking at them. They were curious about the two unlikely strangers who suddenly appeared in their midst. They scooted over and made enough room for Mark and the sergeant to sit on the side of one of their bunks, and listened as Mark explained the series of events that had brought them there.

Occasionally, Mark would take a look out the door of the moving train to see if he could spot their train ahead of them. Now and then he did get a glimpse of it.

He began to notice that their navy troop train would sometimes stop just outside of a town and that, if they looked out the door and up the track, they could see their civilian train. It would stop at the train station about a half of a mile ahead of them. They could see it taking on passengers, and then pull out and continue to the next station. Immediately afterward, their navy train would start up and follow about a mile behind it.

Mark and the sergeant talked it over and decided that at the next stop, they would jump out of the navy boxcar and make a run for the civilian train at the station ahead, and try to catch it. After an hour or so passed, they felt the navy train begin to slow down, so they positioned themselves near the open boxcar door. The moment their train came to a full stop, they jumped down and made a dash for the civilian one. Having just been through cadet training, Mark was in the best physical condition of his life, so didn't mind the running, and was surprised to see the sergeant could keep up with him.

As they approached within two hundred yards of it, the civilian train started to move again. They ran as hard as they could, but it was soon evident that the train was gaining too much speed for them to catch it. To make things worse, they suddenly realized that they would have to turn and run full speed back to the navy train before it started up and left them completely stranded. As they began running back, they could see the sailors leaning out of the boxcars cheering them on: "Come on, Lieutenant! Let's go, Sergeant!" until, at last, they jumped up into a boxcar, gasping for breath and blasting their luck.

In about another hour the navy train began to slow down again, so they repositioned themselves at the open boxcar door. When the train stopped, they jumped out and made another run for it, urged on by the cheering sailors who had, by now, all entered into the spirit of the chase. But again, they missed the forward train and had to scurry back to their boxcar.

On the fourth try, while stopped at Charlotte, North Carolina, they managed to catch the civilian train moments before it pulled out of the station. They found their seats and were relieved to find that their belongings were right where they had left them.

It was late afternoon when Mark finally arrived in Montgomery, Alabama and caught a bus to Selma.

As always, the buses were crowded, and he found himself standing in the aisle.

Then, something happened that he had never witnessed before. A nice-looking lady in her late twenties stood up and offered him her seat! He was completely taken off guard and embarrassed. Back home, he had always offered his seat on the street car to a lady if she were standing, but never the other way around. He tried to refuse this young woman, thanking her ever so much; however, she would not take no for an answer.

So there he was, a number one physical specimen, sitting down while a lady stood. But such was the patriotic spirit of the nation. Civilians often bent over backward for the soldiers they felt would soon be going into combat and risking their lives for them.

CHAPTER 13

(Selma, Alabama; Eglin Field, Florida)

Mark was well aware that the time for his entering combat was rapidly approaching. He had completed the majority of his flying and ground training. What remained now were gunnery and dive-bomb training, and finally learning to fly the airplane that he would actually fly in combat?

At Selma, he would have the thrill of his first flight in a real fighter airplane. It would be a unique experience for two reasons. First, the plane he would fly was a P-40, made famous by Claire Chennault's Flying Tigers in China. It was the plane that had sharks' teeth painted on its nose, giving it a frightening appearance. Second, it would be the first time he would fly an airplane without first having an instructor flying with him. Since the P-40 had only one seat, he would have to go it alone right from the beginning.

The new officers went through thorough, rigorous ground school training where they learned and were tested on all the systems of the airplane, including fuel, hydraulic, electrical, optical, armament, and the engine.

In addition, they had to pass the usual blindfold cockpit check. The pilot would sit in the cockpit with his eyes covered with a blinder while the instructor, standing on the wing, leaned over looking into the cockpit and called out the names of instruments and controls. The pilot was required to touch them quickly: altimeter, oil pressure, flap control, compass, and all the others.

Finally the day came when they were going to actually fly.

As Mark walked out to the flight line and approached the plane assigned to him, he looked up at it and thought it was the biggest plane he had ever seen. It towered over him. The crew chief was standing by as he checked the maintenance record and completed his walk-around inspection. Mark asked him about a couple of the minor write-ups, and was satisfied that they would not interfere with the plane's ability to fly, but he still had a slight feeling of uncertainty as he used the handholds to climb up onto the wing.

I'll have time, he thought to himself, to look around the cockpit once I get in, and gain more confidence.

He strapped himself into the seat and slowly started his cockpit check, going around the cockpit from left to right. He glanced out at the crew chief, who was standing on the ground sweltering in the midsummer, 115-degree heat. He was looking up at Mark, hopeful that he would start the plane without too much delay so that he could get out of the hot sun and back into the shade somewhere. So Mark completed his check a bit quicker than he would have liked, and yelled "Clear!" The crew chief signaled back that the prop was clear and that it was okay for him to start his engine.

The Allison engine started smoothly, though with a certain amount of crackling and popping that was characteristic of that particular engine.

So far, so good, he thought. Now I'll look around the cockpit a bit and gain more confidence before taxiing out for take-off.

He turned his radio on, and could hear the tower talking to airplanes taking off and coming in for landings. Suddenly he was startled by the sound of his instructor's voice over the radio yelling, "Number 293! Get that plane moving before it overheats!" Mark suddenly realized that his instructor was in the tower, yelling at him.

He glanced down at his temperature gauge, and sure enough, it was starting to climb rather rapidly. He looked out at the sweltering, impatient crew chief and noticed his relief when he gave him the signal to remove the chocks.

He got permission from the tower to taxi for take-off, and started taxiing out of the parking area and down the taxi strip that lead toward the end of the runway. As with most fighters, the large nose loomed up in front of him, blocking the view straight ahead, making it necessary for the pilot to taxi in S-turns so that the pilot could see forward, first out of one side of the open canopy and then the other.

Okay, now I can look around a bit, he thought, and try to get a little more confident with this thing, before I take off.

As he pulled up near the end of the runway and started to look around again, his instructor's voice once again boomed out over the radio. "293, get that plane off the ground before it over-heats!"

So without further adieu, and with a persistent feeling of uncertainty, Mark got permission for take-off, taxied out to take-off position, locked the tail wheel, and eased the throttle full forward.

The surge of power seemed incredible compared to the trainers he had been flying up to that time, and he could feel the acceleration pushing him back against his seat. As the airplane continued to accelerate, he kept it lined up by keeping the same amount of runway visible on each side of the nose which was still blocking out his forward vision. As the plane picked up speed and the tail wheel lifted, his forward vision improved.

The plane quickly approached take-off speed, and he eased the stick back and felt the wheels leave the ground. He raised the landing gear, reached up with one hand and pulled the canopy closed, and started his climb.

Wow! What a sensation! He looked around to make sure the area was clear of other airplanes, and then started a climbing turn. As he glanced around the cockpit, he started to settle down a bit, and was amazed to see that he was already passing through two thousand feet.

He continued climbing to ten thousand feet and looked down along the long, slim nose cowling which covered the in-line liquid-cooled Allison engine. The engine purred smoothly.

His first inclination was to try a roll. The simplest one to do was a barrel roll, so he pulled the nose up a bit and then moved the stick over to one side. The airplane started spinning like a top around its pointed nose. He stopped the roll after three turns and was delighted with the ease of execution of the maneuver. The airplane felt as if it could roll all day with very little effort.

He did some climbs, and some power-on and power-off stalls, so that he could see how it would feel when he came in for a landing. He then put the airplane into a slight dive to build up speed, and did a loop. Now satisfied that he had a pretty good feel of how the plane handled, he flew around the local area to become familiar with the Alabama landscape.

When he finally turned back to return to the airfield, he was startled to see oil splattering and beginning to cover his windshield. It seemed to be coming from the side of the engine and was making it almost impossible for him to see forward through the windshield. He immediately called the tower and requested an emergency landing.

The tower asked him, "What is your problem?"

"I've got oil covering my windshield and almost zero forward visibility."

The tower seemed to take his dilemma rather calmly and cleared him for landing on runway 27.

As he approached his downwind leg, he slid the canopy open and had no trouble keeping the runway in sight. He could still keep it in sight as he turned onto the downwind leg and then onto the base leg. But as he turned onto final, the runway disappeared behind the oil-covered windshield.

The only way he could keep the runway in sight was to slip the airplane as he flew down the final approach. It was a cross-controlled, uncoordinated maneuver, with the stick trying to turn the plane one way and the rudder trying to turn it the opposite way. The result was that the plane flew slightly sideways during its descent. There was some danger to the maneuver, especially in an unfamiliar airplane, because of the possibility of stalling. However, it did turn the nose of the airplane slightly to the right as he slipped down toward his left, and he was able to keep the runway in sight out of the left side of the open canopy.

He flew all the way down the final approach in the skid, and just before touching down, leveled off, straightened the nose so that it was aligned in the direction of the runway, and waited for the wheels to hit. The airplane landed surprisingly smoothly, and he was able to take it back to the parking area by "S-ing" it as he taxied.

Mark was still excited as he rushed into the ready room to tell his instructor what happened. However, much to Mark's chagrin, his instructor shrugged and said, "That's a common occurrence in this airplane." Mark couldn't help but feel frustrated. He wondered why, if it happened so often, the instructor didn't mention it during their ground school training, and tell them how to handle the situation when it happens.

Mark was beginning to learn that many things happen while flying that no one ever tells you about ahead of time. I guess that's the reason why the Air Corps put us through all those mental, physical, coordination and reaction tests when selecting pilots, thought Mark. They want to get men who can react quickly to the unexpected.

After a few weeks of flying the P-40, they were sent by bus to Eglin field for gunnery training. Eglin was a huge air base in Florida that had many airstrips scattered throughout. His group was assigned to a remote strip where they would learn both aerial and ground gunnery.

It was very quiet and peaceful there. They had their own little airstrip to themselves, and it gave Mark the feeling of being alone on a remote island somewhere.

After some classroom instruction, the morning arrived when he was going to fly his first air-to-ground gunnery flight. The airplane they would be using was the AT-6 Texan, the same kind they used in advanced flying training, except that these had a machine gun mounted on their noses. Mark walked out on the flight line to the airplane which was assigned to him, and started his walk-around check before getting into it.

The check included looking for any damage to the wing, tail, control surfaces, and landing gear, and making sure there were no nicks in the propeller. Imagine his surprise when, upon inspecting the propeller, he not only found a nick, but an actual bullet hole through the propeller! He immediately started walking back to the operations shack, and was surprised when he saw his instructor walking out to meet him.

"What's the problem?" he asked.

"I can't fly that airplane. It's got a bullet hole in the prop."

"So do most of the planes out here," he replied. "Don't let that bother you. It'll fly okay."

Mark knew that the machine gun in the nose was synchronized to fire through the propeller without hitting it. His instructor explained that sometimes it would get a bit out of sync, or sometimes a round sitting in the hot barrel of a gun that had just been firing a long burst, would "cook" off. The only noticeable effect was a whistling sound as the propeller increased its speed during take-off.

Mark took off and joined up with three of the other student pilots. They were flying to the gunnery range in formation, with their instructor in the lead. Upon reaching the target area, the instructor told them that he would show them how to make a strafing pass at the target.

The targets consisted of a row of panels mounted at an angle on frames on the ground and facing slightly upward. They were each assigned to one of the panels and were to dive at it from eight hundred feet, and fly so as to bring the target into their gun sight. Then they fired a burst at it, trying to get as many hits as possible before they had to pull up in time to keep from flying into the ground.

As Mark took his turn at the strafing runs, he found them to be some of the most exciting, and probably the most dangerous, flying that he had done so far. All through flight training the pilots had constantly been told not to fly below a thousand feet, except for take-offs and landings, and never to do acrobatics below five thousand feet in a small plane, or fifteen thousand feet in a fighter. Now here they were, starting their steep strafing runs at about eight hundred feet and diving toward the ground while firing at the target, to probably within one or two hundred feet of the target, then pulling up into a steep climb before hitting the ground. He looked back over his shoulder at the target as he climbed away from it. He then reentered the pattern for another pass. As they grew more experienced and more daring, their pull-ups became steeper and ended up being almost a half-loop off the deck, with a roll-out on top. Mark felt it was very exciting.

The training at Eglin and Selma soon grew to a close, and Mark knew that the day was quickly approaching when the pilots would be entering combat. It was a frightening thought, full of unknowns and brimming with terrifying possibilities, yet Mark had resigned himself to it, and his commitment to entering combat never wavered.

CHAPTER 14

(Goldsboro, North Carolina)

Mark was finally going to get checked out, and gain confidence in the airplane he would fly in combat. The P-47 Thunderbolt was the newest and largest of the United States' fighters in production. It was different from most fighters in that it had a built-in turbo supercharger that enabled it to perform better at higher altitudes than most airplanes, but its air-cooled engine and eight machine guns also made it very effective at lower altitudes.

He was sent to the southern town of Goldsboro, North Carolina, for his initial check-out, and training flights.

At Goldsboro, he was treated more like an officer than ever before, and he had the freedom to go to town whenever he finished training for the day. John Bradley and Don Ballenger were Mark's roommates. They had been through most of their flying training together and, in spite of their differences in personalities, got along well, often going into town together. Don's frequent smiles reflected his happy-go-lucky attitude. John, the deep thinker of the three, was quieter but congenial, and a good friend. Mark, who was always a bit in awe of learning to fly and still found it hard to believe he was a soldier, treasured their friendship.

One Saturday, when the three of them were lying around the barracks wondering what to do with themselves, Don suggested that they try hitchhiking somewhere.

They all agreed and soon were out on the side of the road, next to the base, trying to catch a ride. An officer hitchhiking during peacetime would be unheard of, but now, with the war in its third year, and with the shortage of automobiles and other forms of transportation, it was being tolerated. By the same token, because of the gas shortage, there was very little traffic on the roads. Eventually, a car did come by and stopped in front of them. It was a Chevy sedan driven by a man in his late twenties.

"Where are you fellows going?" he asked.

"Anywhere you are," they responded.

"I'm going to Wilson."

"That's fine with us."

"Hop in."

Soon they were on their way going somewhere north. The man was a very pleasant fellow, said that his name was Tom Billingsly, and was a photographer on his way to an assignment in Wilson.

The three of them had no idea where Wilson was, nor did they care. It was a nice day and a pleasant ride.

Tom then looked at them out of the corner of his eye and with a slight smile said, "I'm going to photograph a beauty contest." Then after a short pause, he added, "You fellows can come along if you want to."

Needless to say they couldn't believe their ears! "Are you kidding? Of course we want to go!" they said.

Tom laughed and went on to elaborate.

A local country club held a beauty contest every year, and it had acquired quite a bit of fame. He went on to explain that the winner of the contest two years before was a girl named Ava Gardner, and she had gone on to become a movie star.

"Wow!" said Mark and his friends.

After driving for almost an hour, Tom turned off the highway and onto a winding road leading up to the country club. They soon found themselves talking to four absolutely gorgeous girls in bathing suits. Tom went on to explain that this was not the contest itself, but just a publicity photo session associated with the contest. He then asked, "Would you fellows mind posing with the girls?"

They jokingly said, "No way," then rushed over to get in line to pose with the girls. Tom took a number of pictures around the pool, and needless to say, the boys were delighted to oblige. They got talking to the girls, hoping to get better acquainted, when Tom came up with another surprise.

"Well, fellows, I am through with the picture taking here, but I am going to photograph a Greek wedding in Wilson this evening, and I'm sure it would be all right if you pilots came along with me if you'd like."

Again, they were delighted with the unexpected invitation.

They asked the girls if they would go with them, and two of them accepted. The others couldn't for various reasons. Leslie Scott agreed to go with Mark.

They ended up not going to the wedding itself, but to the reception following the wedding, which was being held in a rented hall. They were warmly welcomed into the group and it turned into a great time, with lots of food, wine, music, and laughter.

Mark was fascinated with the Greek folk dances in which the men formed a line with their arms around the shoulders of the men next to them. They moved slowly sideways in time with the music, dipping every so often as they maneuvered across the floor. At one point, the man at the head of the line hung from a hand-kerchief being held by the man next to him, and he bent and twirled on one foot, as he swung under the other man's arm. Everyone seemed to be having a lot of fun, laughing, clapping, and shouting; the next thing Mark knew, he was up there dancing, hanging from the handkerchief and twirling while everyone laughed.

The frustrating part about the whole affair was that the ladies were not dancing. There he was with Leslie, one of the most beautiful girls he had ever seen, and he didn't have a chance to dance with her.

After the party, he talked to Don and John. "I'm going to walk Leslie home, fellas. I'll see you back at the base later." The walk to her house was about twenty minutes. Her home was a comfortable, one-story house with the typical porch swing that almost every southern home had. They sat on her swing and talked for a while. Leslie proved to be not only beautiful, but very intelligent as well, and much to Mark's dismay, his best lines were not making much of an impression on her. There was an open screened window next to the swing and Mark felt sure that her mother was on the other side of it, listening to everything they said. He had to be satisfied with some pleasant conversation and a goodnight kiss before leaving to catch a bus back to Goldsboro.

CHAPTER 15

(Goldsboro, North Carolina)

Mark diligently studied all the important parts and features of the P-47 Thunderbolt. He passed his blindfold cockpit check and had now reached the point where he was going to do his first acrobatic flight. He was excited because he wanted to see what this big, powerful fighter could do, yet a bit apprehensive, because in the last three days two pilots had been killed while performing acrobatics.

It was impossible for the instructor to ride in the same plane with the student on his first flight, or on any other flight for that matter, since it was a single- seated fighter.

One morning, Mark and his instructor Lt. Rogers went out to their planes, took off in formation, climbed to 25,000 feet, and leveled off. They flew to a sparsely-inhabited area where the loud noises they would be making wouldn't cause residents much disturbance, and a crash wouldn't be likely to kill anybody.

They circled the area once to make sure there were no other airplanes around. When satisfied that they were clear, Lt. Rogers looked through his canopy at Mark, and signaled that he was going to do his first maneuver. He pulled off to the right and did a roll to the right, then waggled his wings as a signal for Mark to perform the same maneuver. Using the same procedure they did a roll to the left, some loops, inverted flight, and power on and power off stalls.

They flew together for a few minutes, making sure the area was still clear for their next maneuver. Lt. Rogers pulled over about three wing lengths away from Mark and started the next maneuver. He rolled his plane upside down, and then pulled his nose straight down through the horizon and into a dive. While diving straight down, he did a spin to the right. He then pulled his plane out of the dive and started climbing back to altitude. As he climbed straight up, he did a spin to the left. Upon reaching 25,000 feet, he joined Mark and waggled his wings for Mark to do the same maneuver.

"Wow!" said Mark.

Mark was impressed with the instructor's performance and peeled away to attempt the same maneuver. He remembered their lectures on the dangers of high-speed dives—how a pilot could easily find himself in a situation where the plane was going so fast that it was impossible for him to complete the pull-up without hitting the ground.

Mark did his wing-over and went into the steep dive. The airspeed indicator started winding up as his speed increased, and the altimeter started winding down as he plunged toward the earth. He watched the matrix of fields, fences, roads, farms, and woods spinning beneath him as he executed his roll going down and was anxious to start his pull-up. He pulled back hard on the stick as he swung through the bottom of his dive, pulling ten "gs." The centrifugal force on his body made all his body parts weigh ten times what they normally weighed on the ground. It also pulled the blood from his brain, causing him to temporarily black out. It was as if two little black curtains came down across his eyes due to the blood being pulled away from his head. Although his eyesight was the first thing to go, he was still aware of what was going on and regained his sight as he released back pressure on the stick as he started to climb. He glanced at his instruments. They were now winding in the opposite direction: the altimeter wound up, and the airspeed wound down.

He was now climbing and went into his slow roll going straight up. As he finished his roll and tried to level off, something strange and frightening happened. The stick and the rudder pedals went limp. Mark flopped them around effortlessly and the airplane gave no response. Suddenly sheer fright smacked him right in the pit of his stomach. There he was with the nose pointing straight up and the airplane stalled completely out of airspeed. It was a helpless feeling, and suddenly he knew what had happened to the two pilots who had been killed a few days earlier.

Next, something happened which seemed to defy explanation. The stick, which had been limp, suddenly shot out of Mark's hand into the full forward position. It took him a moment to realize that the plane was sliding down backward, tail first, and the force of the air pressing against the elevator had forced the stick forward!

Mark was beginning to go through the bail-out procedures. He had never heard of anyone being in this situation before, and wasn't sure what to do. It seemed that there was no alternative. If he couldn't control the plane, he just couldn't sit there as it fell to earth.

He started reaching up to open the canopy so that he could bail out, but just as his hand touched the canopy handle, he became aware of a little firmness developing on the right rudder pedal. He brought his hand back, and decided to stay with the plane a little while longer. He wanted to see if he could regain some control of the airplane, which seemed to have become nothing more than seven tons of falling metal.

The rudder pressure was beginning to build up, and the nose of the plane began to move away from the vertical and fall off to the right. Mark knew that the greatest effort at this point was to keep the plane from entering an inverted spin. In this type of spin, the pilot is upside down on his back and the plane goes into a flat spin, a situation from which no one had been known to recover.

As he continued holding the right rudder in, the nose kept falling off more and more to the right. To Mark's relief, he saw it come down through the horizon. He now started feeling some stick pressure coming back, and knew he had recovered safely.

The next time he attempted this maneuver, he would be sure to let the airspeed build up higher in the dive, and then lose no time pulling up and quickly completing his vertical roll so that he would still have enough airspeed left to fly the plane and recover.

* * * *

"Mark, our roommate Don Ballinger has had an accident." John said he had just heard about it and didn't know the details. "Apparently he survived it okay, but he's now in the hospital recovering from his injuries."

They went to visit Don that evening at the local hospital. He was lying in the hospital bed with a big bandage around his head. He appeared a bit groggy, but was able to smile. He was obviously pleased to see his roommates visit him.

After a few minutes, he started telling them about his accident.

"I had been flying for two hours and was returning to the base when my engine started acting up and finally quit. I desperately looked for a place to belly in, and spotted a farmer's field about 5 miles from the base. It was a rough landing and I got bounced around quite a bit and slid to a stop just before hitting the barn. As the airplane was sliding, I jumped out and started running away to get as far from it as possible. I had heard that airplanes sometimes blew up if the fuel lines ruptured. When I reached a tree a few hundred yards away, I sat down under it and tried to compose myself. I looked back at my plane. It was lying there on its belly, with its props bent backward.

"When I took off my helmet and brushed my hair back with my hand, I noticed it was covered with blood. I began to realize that my head was bleeding quite badly, and started to get a bit panicky. I remembered that the airplane carried a small first aid kit attached to the inside of the cockpit, just below the canopy, so

I ran back to the plane, climbed up on the wing, and reached inside the open canopy. I tried to unsnap the first aid pouch from its mounting, but couldn't get it to come loose. Those two snaps that hold it on are very strong.

"When I started to taste the blood that was running down my face, in sheer desperation I gave the pouch a yank and tore it loose from the airplane.

"As I staggered back to the tree, the farmer's wife came running up to help me. She had seen the crash and raced to the scene as quickly as she could. She bandaged my head and then ran home to call an ambulance."

Later, Mark and John went out to an airplane and tried pulling a first aid kit off the way Don had. It was designed to release easily if you pulled it in one direction, but was almost impossible to release if you pulled it in the other direction. They were unable to pull it free no matter how hard they tried. It drove home a point to Mark that he had heard before: A person is sometimes able to muster up almost superhuman strength in the face of panic.

Don was kept in the hospital for a week and then released back to duty.

CHAPTER 16

(Dover, Delaware)

Mark was transferred to Dover, Delaware for his final training before going to combat.

The next three weeks of training were hectic. They practiced air-to-ground gunnery, air-to-air gunnery, and dive-bombing. Their first flights were usually at eight o'clock in the morning, followed by ground school, and then a lot of sitting around and waiting. They were usually released at four o'clock.

Mark's mother lived in Wilmington, which was only 45 miles away from the base. His father had died four months before and he missed him very much.

He decided to call Joanne and ask her if she could come to stay with his mother while he was at Dover. That way, he could drive up to see her several times a week before leaving for combat. He was pleasantly surprised to find that she wanted to do it, but was not sure her parents would agree.

Joanne's parents, who lived on a very tight budget, finally agreed to send her for a two-week visit.

It was wonderful having her so close, yet somewhat frustrating not being able to see her every day. Gas rationing limited his trips home to once during the week, and again on weekends. Mark would drive home as quickly as possible, and stay as long as possible, trying to squeeze in every minute he could for their time together.

His mother usually prepared a nice dinner, and then he and Joanne would go dancing or to a movie. They would also park down on Cleaver Farm Road, necking and talking until two or three in the morning. Joanne slept in his room, and he slept on the couch in the living room.

There was no doubt that Joanne had marriage on her mind, and so did Mark, but he was determined to wait until after the war—when and if he came back from combat.

During her second week at his mom's house, they drove to a small train station. It was a whistle stop out in the country, and no one was there. They kissed and talked. They were now to the point where she allowed him to get intimate. Mark even suspected that if he pressured her, she would allow him to go further. But for the first time in his life, the feeling that this was the girl he would marry overrode his lust. He restrained himself from engaging in the ultimate act, wanting to wait until after they were wedded. He felt it would give special meaning to the word "marriage."

That night, he asked her if she would wait for him, and marry him when he returned from the war. She said, "Yes." He fumbled in his pocket for a small box that he had managed to keep a secret all night. He opened it to reveal a gold ring with a small diamond. She eagerly put it on her finger and looked at it lovingly with a smile. They were engaged.

They were both blissfully happy at that moment, but it was getting to be almost two o'clock Monday morning, and he had to be on the flight line at seven, so he took her home, said goodnight, and then drove lickety-split down the highway to Dover. He arrived at the base about quarter past four in the morning, set his alarm clock for six, flopped into bed, and got about an hour's sleep.

When the clock went off, he was bleary-eyed and having a terrible time waking up, but he grabbed a quick breakfast and rushed to the flight line for his seven o'clock briefing.

They were told that they would be practicing ground gunnery in flights of six planes that morning.

Mark climbed into his airplane, practically walking in his sleep, and took off to join the rest of the formation, flying out to the target area at two thousand feet.

As they flew, Mark kept banging his head against the headrest mounted to the armored plate behind his seat, trying to stay awake, but in spite of all his efforts, he caught himself starting to doze. It startled him so much that he turned his oxygen regulator up to a hundred percent, and doubled his efforts to stay awake.

They reached the target area and could see the target panels lined up on the ground like a group of large paintings mounted on rigid, artists' easels facing up at an angle. Instead of paintings, however, there were large numbers from one to ten stenciled on the canvasses. Their instructor assigned each of them a target by number.

They flew a rectangular pattern from which they dove at their assigned targets in turn and tried to get as many hits as possible before pulling up. They each had two hundred rounds of ammunition, and could fire about twenty to forty rounds on each pass. It seemed to Mark that the flight would never end. He shot longer bursts than usual because he was trying to use up his ammo faster—hopefully making their flight end sooner. But even though his ammo was gone, he still had to stay with the flight until the last pilot had finished. That was one hour that seemed like three days to him.

When they finally returned to the flight line, he staggered out of his plane and could only think of trying to get back to his room for an hour's nap. He noticed that the captain in charge of their group's training was walking toward him as he climbed down from the plane. As he approached Mark, he asked, "What'd you do with the other seven shots?"

Mark was a bit startled, and wondered what he was talking about. "What do you mean?" he asked, trying to bring his fuzzy mind into focus.

"You got a hundred and ninety-three hits out there," he said.

Usually we were lucky to get thirty-five or forty hits! Over a hundred was unheard of—yet somehow in his stupor he had broken all gunnery records held up to that time. The only thing he could attribute it to was that in his eagerness to get the mission over with, he had fired longer bursts. That meant that he had flown down closer to the target before pulling up. It had been a very dangerous thing to do. As he thought back, he realized how lucky he had been not to hit the ground.

Mercifully, his flying training at Dover drew to a close. The rigors of staying up most of the night with Joanne, and racing down the highway to fly in the early morning, were wearing him down. He did not feel alert enough to fly carefully, and getting sloppy in a high performance fighter could easily become fatal.

He was given two days to report to the port of embarkation at Camp Kilmer, New Jersey.

He took Joanne to the train station to catch her return trip home to Jackson. It was evening. Half a dozen other soldiers were saying good-bye to their girlfriends and wives on the platform.

As they kissed for the last time, Joanne reached into her purse and pulled something out. "Here," she said. "It's something brought along for you just in case we had decided to get married."

Mark looked down at what she held in her fingers. It was a gold wedding band.

"Please marry me," she said.

He felt embarrassed, but he looked at her and said, "I can't now. There are too many uncertainties. I might get wounded in combat and become a burden to you the rest of your life."

She paused, and then said, "I want you to have it anyway. Please wear it."

He took it and placed it on the second finger of his right hand. "I'll wear it there until I return," he promised. "Then when we get married, you can move it to my left hand."

They kissed again for the last time, and she boarded the train.

CHAPTER 17

(New York Harbor, New York)

After several months of learning how to fly and fight with the P-47 Thunderbolt, Mark was sent to an army base in the New York Harbor. There he would be processed and shipped to a combat zone. As always, neither he nor anyone else had any idea where they would be shipped to, or how long they would be at sea getting there.

The smoke-filled officers' club at Camp Kilmer was packed and noisy. Among the crowd was a movie star who, like the rest of them, was waiting to embark and sail to his overseas assignment. Someone said it was Jimmy Stewart, but Mark never did see him. It was definitely a time of excitement, as well as apprehension.

The mood was festive, and there was no sign of gloom over the possible fate that loomed before them. They had all been training hard and long, yet sometimes the days seemed to drag. At other times they felt a great uncertainty as to their ability to face what they visualized as Hitler's hardened and seasoned pilots and ground troops. They sometimes got the uneasy feeling that they didn't quite get enough of the kind of training they needed to be useful in combat. Actually, none of their instructors had ever been in combat.

Camp Kilmer was named after the poet Joyce Kilmer, who wrote the poem "Trees." Mark learned that he was a soldier in France during World War 1 and was killed in combat.

On the morning of their third day at Kilmer, they found themselves climbing up a gangplank that led to the deck of a large ocean liner. Mark read its name painted on its side near the prow:

The Aquitania. He learned that it had been a British luxury liner in peacetime and was converted to a troop ship when the war started.

Mark was assigned to a cabin that normally slept two, but had been modified to hold four officers.

The ship was jammed full and, of course, no one had any idea where it would take them, as was always the case with combat assignments. Since they were leaving from the east coast, they felt that it would probably be to someplace in Europe or Africa, but if they were needed badly enough, they could be sent through the Panama Canal to the Pacific theater.

The biggest danger on their way would be U-boats. A large troop ship such as theirs would make a wonderful target for the smaller boats.

As they sailed out of the harbor, they couldn't help feeling a lump in their throats when they passed the Statue of Liberty and headed out toward the open sea. Rumor had it that they were to be part of a convoy and escorted by navy destroyers, but there were no other ships in sight.

After Mark settled in and met his roommates, he took a walk around the decks and passageways, and into the communal rooms that were open to them. The Grand Ballroom had been converted to an officers' lounge filled with tables and chairs. It would be their main refuge where they could spend much of their time, talking, playing cards, reading, and writing letters.

Most of the officers were assigned a temporary duty of some sort for the duration of the trip. Mark was given the assignment of "brig officer." He was not told what he was supposed to do as a brig officer, nor even where the brig was, although rumor had it that the brig was somewhere below and toward the bow. Luckily he was never called on to take any action on the job.

The days became routine: rising, eating breakfast, walking around the deck, sitting in the lounge, reading, writing, eating lunch, more reading, card playing, eating supper, more reading, and more card playing. Once in a while he found it pleasant to go out on deck and watch the ship slicing its way through the waves. When the day ended, he went to bed and waited for the next day of the same routine.

The food was surprisingly good, considering the meat shortage back in the States. Many of the ship's peacetime waiters and kitchen staff were still working aboard the ship. Since it was a British ship, they often had fish on the breakfast menu. Mark had never heard of having fish for breakfast, but found that he began to like it.

Except for the nurses' quarters, which were off limits to male passengers, officers and enlisted men were given the run of the ship. One day Mark decided to see what the enlisted quarters were like. It was to be one of the few times that he was very thankful to be an officer. The men's quarters were in the hole of the ship where cargo was normally carried. Cots were stacked three high, with just enough room for a man to slide into one and lie down. Everywhere he looked, he saw row after row of these bunks. Not only was it crowded, the air was so rank and stale that it made him gasp when he entered the large, makeshift room. He felt very sorry for these men who had to endure this dungeon-like life, and felt a little guilty when he climbed back up to the relative luxury of his four-man cabin.

They had been at sea for almost two weeks. Every night, before turning in, he took a walk around the deck and looked at the horizon, but could see nothing but water in every direction. Each morning when he woke up, he went for a walk around the deck before breakfast and, again, saw nothing but water as far as the eye could see. One morning, as he climbed the stairs and stepped out on deck, he was startled to find the ship cruising up a rather narrow passageway with the most beautiful, bright green, grassy rolling hills to either side of it.

Soon everyone was on deck, lined up along the ship's railings, watching the breathtakingly beautiful scenery. Then someone learned that the place was Scotland, and that they were cruising up the Firth of Clyde toward Glasgow.

The scene was made more enchanting by the endless stone walls outlining the fields of the farmlands. There was a strange weather phenomenon, however. Wherever Mark looked, he saw fluffy clouds releasing small showers, but in between the clouds, the sun shone brightly. So as they cruised through the passage, they went in and out of small rain showers. No one seemed to mind because of the pleasant, warm sunshine in between.

As the ship approached Glasgow, they reached what appeared to be a large bay, crowded with military ships of various sorts, including an American aircraft carrier. The water was quite choppy and the carrier seemed to be doing a bit of bobbing up and down. Yet he watched in amazement as airplanes came in and landed on its deck. That had to be one of the most difficult things to do with an airplane, Mark thought. It would be bad enough having to make a perfect landing on a runway that small on dry land, let alone having a postage stamp size airstrip bob up and down as you came down the final approach. He began to feel that they, the army air force pilots, were really spoiled. We always have a runway at least a mile long and it is always rock steady, thought Mark.

They disembarked in Glasgow, but hardly got to see any of the town on their short drive to a large train station. There, they were served coffee and doughnuts by Red Cross women, and then put aboard a train heading south. Their destination turned out to be a large military base used for processing pilots on their way to combat. It was situated on the outskirts of a town called Stoke-on-Trent, which was located near the central part of England. From there, they would be assigned to the fighter group they would be flying with.

The main pastime, while waiting for their new assignments to come through, was gambling in the officers' club—primarily craps. There always seemed to be one guy who was cleaning up at the expense of the others. Back in the States, the chant around a crap game was always "A dollar open! A dollar open!" But here in England, the chant was "A Pound open! A Pound open!" A Pound was worth four dollars, so bets were four times as big, and a man lost his money four times as fast—except for Lt. Hartman, however, who was making it four times as fast. He held a roll of pound notes in one hand that was almost the size of a roll of toilet paper, and rolled the dice with the other hand. It must have been worth over a thousand dollars.

But money was losing much of its meaning now that they were going into combat. The feeling that more or less prevailed was, why worry about it? There was not much to do with one's money anyway, and most of the pilots were sending the maximum amount from their pay that the military allowed, back home to their families or to their banks. In an effort to stem black market trading, the amount they could send to the States was limited to a percentage of their pay. Mark suspected the more imaginative guys found a way of sending larger amounts home. Anyway, like many of the men, Mark thought, I might be dead tomorrow, so why worry about money?

After supper, Mark decided to catch a bus into town to see what Great Britain and the British people were like. The bus took him near the center of town and let him off where he was immediately faced with two problems. It was winter and freezing cold and it was completely dark due to the enforced black-out which was in effect throughout Great Britain. Mark didn't know where to go or how to get there, so he desperately latched on to a group of congenial fellows who were heading to a large dance hall. They walked for about 15 minutes in the dark, following a fellow who apparently had been there before. When they got to the building and opened the door, the light was blinding.

It felt nice to get inside the warm, well-lighted building, and the music sounded good to his ears. The band played the standard Glenn Miller and Tommy Dorsey style music. As Mark watched the couples dancing on the floor, he wondered what British girls would be like.

After watching for a while, he got up enough nerve to ask a girl to dance with him. Although she was a bit stiff, it was pleasant to be dancing with a girl in his arms after being out in the cold. She was nice looking and interesting to talk with, although he sometimes had a bit of trouble understanding some of her choppy speech. He danced with several of the other girls during the evening, but found himself coming back to the first one quite often.

As the end of the dance neared, he told her that he was going to have to leave in order to catch his bus back to the base. She surprised him by saying "I'll walk with you to the bus stop if you like."

"But it's over a mile to the bus stop!"

"That's all right," she said. "I don't mind."

As they walked though the dark, cold night, arm in arm, he couldn't help thinking that no American girl would walk a mile to a bus stop with him under these conditions after a dance.

Mark figured that there were two possibilities as to where he could be sent. One possibility was that he could go to a base somewhere there in England, from which he would fly escort for bombers going on raids into France and Germany. But it had been several months since the Allied forces began their invasion of France on D-Day, and the Germans were slowly being pushed out of France toward the German border. A second possibility seemed more likely: that most of the fighter pilots now entering combat would be sent to France.

CHAPTER 18

(France)

The next day, Mark found himself in the back of a C-47 transport airplane, flying across the English Channel and landing at Le Bourget Airfield. It was the same field that Lindbergh had landed on seventeen years earlier in The Spirit of St Louis when he had just become the first person to fly solo across the Atlantic Ocean.

Mark and eight other pilots got out of the plane, and loaded their B-4 bags on to some waiting trucks. They were then driven for several hours through the suburbs of Paris, and finally ended up in front of what obviously was once a fine mansion. It was now, however, beginning to show signs of wear and tear due to heavy military usage. Mark soon learned that it was the Chateau de Rothschild. Before the war, it had been the palatial home of Count Rothschild, the rich banking mogul of Europe. Apparently the secret of his wealth was that he used carrier pigeons to communicate with his banks in England. The Germans had been using the mansion, during their occupation of Paris, as their propaganda headquarters. Axis Sal made her broadcasts from there every day, trying to sweet-talk the American GIs into laying down their arms and surrendering to the Germans.

The chateau still had its curved marble staircase and elaborately painted walls and ceilings fairly well intact. All the luxury furnishings, however, had been moved elsewhere, and now the rooms were incongruously furnished with just the necessary rudiments: crude tables and chairs used by the army in processing pilots on their way to their squadrons. One of the largest rooms was used as the mess hall.

There were also still areas around the chateau that were roped off to keep anyone from walking on them. These were areas where the Germans had planted land mines, and the army had not yet taken time to clear them.

Mark ended up staying at the Chateau Rothschild for several days, and was delighted to have a chance to go into Paris before being sent forward to his unit.

Paris had been declared an open city by the French when it was about to be attacked by the advancing Germans. That meant that France was surrendering the city without a fight, thereby sparing it from the bombardment and devastation usually associated with war. Consequently, the city was pretty much as intact as it was in peacetime, showing very little of the signs of the damage that was prevalent everywhere else.

In addition to the city itself, the new pilots were eager to meet the French Mademoiselles about whom they had heard stories from some of the fellows who had arrived before them.

On his second day at the chateau, Mark and some of the other replacement pilots took a bus to the center of Paris. They rode through the suburbs, eager for their first glimpse of the Eiffel Tower and the Arc de Triomphe. The bus drove pasts the two landmarks, giving them a pleasant thrill, and then dropped them off in front of the Opera House. Mark made sure he found out how, when, and where to catch the bus back to the chateau.

Most of the group went their separate ways, but Mark and a pilot named Larry Thomas walked along together. They stopped in front of a café, wondering where to go.

"Mark, there's a kiosk down at the corner. Wait here and I'll try to get us a map. I hope they take American money."

Mark took a seat in the outdoor café, ordered coffee, and waited for Larry. He came back in a few minutes smiling and waving a map. They unfolded the map and started studying it together. It showed the layout of Paris and its different sections.

"We're here," Larry said, as he pointed to the Opera House. "Here's the Eiffel Tower," Mark noted.

They had been told that the area noted for its prostitutes was Pigalle. Curiosity got the best of them and they both agreed it would be an area interesting to explore. With the aid of the map, they found a nearby entrance to the Paris subway system, the "metro." They went downstairs to the platform, looked at the map on the wall, found the number of their train, and soon were on their way to Pigalle.

When they reached their station, they climbed the stairs to the surface street and found themselves in the midst of the Pigalle area. They walked down the street, passing the Moulin Rouge night club, where Toulouse-Lautrec had sketched his famous pictures of the Cancan girls.

They didn't encounter any prostitutes walking down the main street, so they turned onto a side street. They soon passed several doorways in which ladies were standing in an inviting fashion.

Mark had never had a sexual encounter with a prostitute, nor had he ever even seen one for that matter. The thought of paying for sex seemed to go against his grain for some reason, even though he had enough money and the cost was not important to him.

As he walked past several doorways, he came upon one girl who had a certain charm about her. She was very different in looks and in manner from any American girl he had ever known, and he found himself stopping and talking to her.

She asked him if he wanted to go upstairs with her. The thought of having a beautiful woman such as her, without having to spend endless time wooing her, suddenly seemed intriguing.

"How much?" he asked, and when she told him, he hesitated for a moment. Not because of the price—it was reasonable enough—but because he was now treading in territory that he had never been in before, and he felt a bit uneasy about it.

He looked at her deep, pensive eyes and her full lips. He looked down at her breasts pressing against her blouse, and at her slim waist and graceful hips. He said yes.

As she led the way up the narrow stairs, he found himself watching her lovely figure as it swayed gracefully from side to side. They entered the small bedroom, and he took her into his arms from behind and reached around, and pressed his hands against her breasts. She didn't object, but then slowly turned around and indicated that he should pay first. He took the money from his wallet, handed it to her, and she walked over to the dresser and put it into her purse.

Mark watched every move she made with fascination. He could not believe that this girl was his, and that she would give herself to him for such a small amount of money.

She started undressing, and then so did he. She was lovely and had a very nice way about her. When they got into bed, he immediately started embracing and kissing her. As she lay there, her hand slid down and started stroking him gently. Then she slid down and performed oral sex, sending shivers through him. As much as he was enjoying it, he wanted to seduce her, so he moved around on top of her. In a few minutes it was over, and they were dressing. As they walked down the steps and back to the doorway, he reached over and gave her one more caress, and then said good-bye.

As he left, he turned to look back at her, and noticed that she was already talking to another soldier. What had been a milestone in his life was obviously only a fleeting moment in hers.

CHAPTER 19

(France)

Upon returning to the chateau that evening, Mark learned that the time had finally arrived for him to go to the front. He would leave to join his squadron in the morning, right after breakfast.

It had been snowing off and on over the last few days, and the weather had suddenly turned much colder. There was some delay in getting off early, but about eleven o'clock, Mark and thirteen other fighter pilots were loaded into the back of a GI truck, along with their B-4 bags. They were each given a box of C-rations to take with them, and carried water in their canteens strapped to their web belts.

Their truck was a standard GI one with a canvas top, but no covering over the back end. It offered very little protection from the icy wind that blew through the gaps in the canvas and out the large opening at the rear of the truck. Mark could instantly tell when they drove out of the pristine area of Paris because their truck suddenly started bouncing and shaking. They were now beginning to feel the effects of the war for the first time. The small town they were now going through was not offered the same protection as Paris, and obviously suffered severe damage to its roads and buildings. As a result of shelling and bombing damage, as well as wear and tear from passing tanks and other heavy military equipment, there was rubble everywhere, and many potholes littered the road. The wooden, slatted seats of the truck seemed to amplify every bump the truck hit. With the constant jarring, and the cold wind swirling in through the large opening in the rear of the truck, it didn't take long for the cold to penetrate Mark's clothing. He soon felt frozen to the bone. The pilots began huddling closer together, trying to keep warm by conserving body heat.

After two hours of complete misery, the truck stopped. The driver got out, walked back to them, and said that he was taking a break so that they could eat lunch: namely the C-rations they had been given beforehand.

The boxes containing C-rations consisted of crackers, a very hard chocolate bar, and a small can of prepared food, which was often cold scrambled eggs laced with tiny pieces of bacon, or a can of Spam, or with any luck, Mark's favorite: corned beef. He walked around the rubble looking for a spot he could use as a table and settled on a windowsill of a partially-destroyed brick building. His can of C-rations contained cold scrambled eggs and bacon. Mark devoured it, and even though it was cold, it tasted good. The best part of the stop, however, was the large thermos of hot coffee that the driver had brought with him from the chateau. He gave each of them a canteen cup full. There was something about the metal canteen cup that defied explanation. To Mark, the cup would always seem to be hotter than its contents, and always manage to burn his lips when he sipped it. The hot liquid was welcome, however, and the heat felt good as it went down, and permeated through his body.

They got back into the truck and the driver drove for four more painful hours. The pilots had no idea where they were going. Since they were so accustomed to not knowing their destination during any military move, it never occurred to them to ask their driver. He obviously knew where he was going since he had to take them there.

Mark could not remember ever being more miserable in his life, and as it grew darker, it grew even colder. He finally sensed the truck turning off the main road onto what seemed to be a county dirt road. This gave him hope that they were approaching their destination. After another half hour of jarring and freezing they pulled to a stop in front of a long, narrow, wooden building. The driver announced that this was the 510th Fighter Squadron, and read off the names of the four pilots who were to get off there. Mark was not one of them.

The truck started up and continued for another ten minutes, apparently driving to another part of the same airfield, and stopped again in front of a similar type building. The driver said that this was the 511th Fighter Squadron and proceeded to call four more names. This time, Mark's was one of them.

The four replacement pilots dismounted and carried their B-4 bags into the wooden building, which was filled with pilots, and smoke, and a potbellied stove radiating generous quantities of heat.

They were greeted by Captain Kolowski, who said that he was the operations officer of the squadron, and he in turn introduced them to Major Adams, the commanding officer. Mark couldn't help overhearing one of them say, "Look how young they're sending 'em up here now."

He was next introduced to his flight leader, Lt. Don Martin. Mark was pleased to meet the men he would soon be flying with, and who seemed friendly enough in a reserved sort of way. But by far the nicest thing in the room was the black, potbellied stove radiating warmth.

After they ate chow in the mess tent, he again met with Lt. Martin. He went on to tell Mark that their fighter group, the 405th, was stationed outside the town of Saint Dizier, France, which was about halfway between Paris and the German border. The Germans were slowly being pushed out of France, but they still occupied the important French cities of Nancy and Metz.

He described the squadron's mission that day had been dive-bombing the fortification around Metz, and said some of their bombs had bounced off the concrete structures and exploded harmlessly in the air, but that they did inflict some damage to the fortress.

"Mark, tomorrow I want you to take an airplane up in the morning and fly around our part of France for a couple of hours to familiarize yourself with the local landscape. That way, if you ever get separated from the squadron during a mission, it will help you find your way back to your home base."

Mark was next introduced to Lt. Frank Easterly, who would be his tent mate. Frank was from Pennsylvania, and had been with the squadron for three months. He was friendly but quiet. He told Mark a bit about the squadron and their recent missions. He went on to explain that their primary mission was to support General Patton's Third Army in their forward drive into Germany. They would dive-bomb and strafe troops, trucks, trains, tanks, fuel and ammunition dumps and any other military target that was assigned to them. They would also enter into air-to-air combat with Nazi fighters whenever the occasion arose.

Frank took him down a partly snow-covered winding path to show him their tent: a pyramid type with a wooden floor. It contained two cots, two chairs, and a potbellied stove. It was winter and nights were very cold. Each tent was allotted a bucketful of coal a day. They could use it whenever they wanted to, but most pilots saved it for the evening so that they could write letters by it, or use it to heat water for bathing, shaving and laundry. A bed roll, two blankets, and a mummy bag were lying on Mark's cot. Frank showed him how to fold the blankets around the mummy bag, in what he called a Boy Scout fold, so that they would fit into the sleeping bag. Mark appreciated all the effort Frank was going through to make him feel welcome.

Lt. Martin had told Mark that combat briefing was at six in the morning, and that he wanted him to attend even though he wouldn't be going on the mission. With that in mind, and the fact that Mark was tired after his long, hard day, he was ready to turn in early. He shimmied into the mummy bag inside the blankets which were inside the bed roll, and felt like a worm sliding into a tight-fitting cocoon. Once in, he pulled the hood over his head and face so that very little but his nose stuck out he fell fast asleep

CHAPTER 20

(Saint Dizier, France)

The sound of reveille being played over a loud speaker fastened to a pole near the center of their camp woke everybody up at five o'clock the next morning.   Reluctantly Mark squirmed through his layers of mummy bags, blankets, and sleeping bag to work a hand up to the zipper at the opening. He felt a shiver go through him as his hand came in contact with a crust of ice which had formed where his breath had frozen on it during the night. He looked at his clothes and pistol hanging on the chair next to his cot. Getting out of his nice warm sleeping bag and stepping onto the ice cold tent floor took all the willpower he could muster.

His tent mate, Frank, had gotten up and dressed a bit faster than Mark, but waited for him to catch up. The freezing morning air and cold tent floor helped him dress in record time.

They left their tent and walked through the dark down the crunchy gravel pathway which was partly covered with new snow. The path wandered around the array of tents and shacks that formed their camp, and finally led to the briefing room located in a partially-destroyed hangar near the flight line.

Sergeant Maynard had gotten up a half hour earlier than anyone else and started a fire in the potbellied stove located in the back of the ready room. It was the only island of warmth to be found in the entire camp at that time of morning. Many of the pilots were already there, and the rest were quietly arriving.

Mark lingered at the stove, standing as close to it as he could, savoring the wonderful warmth it emitted. He started to smell something burning. When he looked down he saw that his pant legs had touched the brim of the stove and started to singe.

His trousers ended up with two small brown burnt marks at the mid-shin level. He also noticed that some of the other pilots had similar tell-tale markings.

"Attention!" someone barked as Major Adams, their commanding officer, entered the room. He took a seat up front that had been saved for him.

Mark inconspicuously took a seat at the back of the room, and Frank sat beside him. A rather tall captain wearing a brown knit sweater under his fleece lined jacket stood up and started his briefing.

"That's Lt. Radcliff, our intelligence officer," Frank explained.

He was in front of a large map which was pinned to the wall behind him, and he twirled his wooden pointer as he spoke. The map was covered with a large sheet of plastic on which several dark lines were drawn.

"Your primary target for today will be in the area of Saar Lauten."

As he spoke he turned to the map and struck it with his pointer. He circled a small town and then adjusted to point specifically to some fuel storage tanks that were located near the north end of the town.

"There is a concentration of Nazis here trying to hold on to this precious fuel supply, so you can expect lots of antiaircraft fire."

As Lt. Radcliff sat down, Capt. Kolowski the operations officer stood and took his place at the map. He was wearing his flight suit with his fleece-lined jacket, and his crushed hat cocked a bit to one side.

"In addition to the fuel dump, we will be looking for targets of opportunity which might help the ground troops in their forward push. The black line represents the front as it existed last night. We normally allow 5 miles to the front of it where we won' bomb or strafe because of the uncertainty of our troop movements. However, as always, with General Patton's Third Army and his often surprising forward thrusts, we will allow a 10 mile safety zone."

Frank leaned over and whispered to Mark.

"He's going into a bit more detail today for the benefit of you new pilots who arrived yesterday."

"We will be three flights of four airplanes each. We will carry a 500-pound bomb under each wing. Our guns will have a mixture of armor piercing and tracer bullets. We will start our engines at 7:45. Let's synchronize our watches. It will be exactly 7:05 when I say hack." The pilots all set their watches to 7:05 and then pulled out their watch stems to stop movement of the hands. The captain then started his countdown.

"Minus 4 seconds, minus 3, minus 2, minus 1, hack."

At the command "hack," all the pilots pushed in the stems of their watches, so they would all be running at the same time.

"Your safe course back to the base if you get separated from the squadron will be 263 degrees."

The pilots all wrote this number on the back of their hand in ink.

Frank explained to Mark, "That way, if they got shot down, they could lick the number off their hand and the enemy would not be able to tell where they came from."

"Your planes and positions are posted on the assignment board."

The briefing ended and each pilot stopped to look at the assignment board for his position. They then went to the mess tent for a quick breakfast.

When they finished eating, the pilots who were flying the morning mission went to their lockers next to the ready room and put on their flight jackets, their shoulder holsters which held their .45 pistols, and slid their escape kits into the knee pockets of their flight suits. The escape kit was a flat plastic case that contained a cloth map of their area of Europe which could also be used as a sling if they broke their arm, a nutritious bar of chocolate, a hack saw blade and a small compass.

They then put on their parachutes, piled on to Jeeps, and were driven through the cold, muddy slush to their airplanes. All the crew chiefs had gotten there much earlier to check out the planes, and stood by waiting for the pilots to arrive. The pilots checked the condition of their airplanes with their crew chiefs, then got into their planes and sat waiting for their watch to reach the appointed time. At exactly 7:45, the silence of the morning was shattered with the roar of sixteen P-47 Thunderbolt engines starting at the same time. It was almost deafening.

After the planes left for their mission, Mark walked back to the pilot shack with Frank and had a cup of coffee. Frank explained to Mark that two missions were flown each day if weather permitted. The same planes were used for both missions if they had not been shot down, or suffered battle damage during the earlier mission. One set of pilots flew in the morning and another in the afternoon. Although the squadron was assigned fifty pilots, the number of planes in condition to fly combat most days was usually twelve to sixteen at any one time.

Frank was scheduled to fly on the next mission.

CHAPTER 21

(Saint Dizier, France)

Mark watched the squadron take off for its morning mission. Now it was time for him to fly his familiarization flight. He went to the locker room to get his parachute, helmet, mask, and maps. He got one of the mechanics to drive him out to the flight line to find the airplane he was assigned to fly.

"Good morning, Sarge. How's the plane this morning?"

"Good morning, sir. We repaired a small flak hole in the tail section last night. The rest of it looks fine."

Mark scrutinized the latest entries in the maintenance book and asked Sergeant Bentley about two of them. Satisfied with his explanation, he started walking around the plane, looking at the surfaces of the wings, the fuselage, and the propeller. He tested the movements of the tail and ailerons. Finally, he kicked the tires to convince himself that they were inflated enough to survive a good landing.

Satisfied with the exterior, Mark climbed into the cockpit and looked at the instrument panel. He checked and adjusted the position of the mixture control, the throttle, the flap settings, the trim tabs, and the free movement of the stick and rudder pedals. Sergeant Bentley helped him buckle his parachute straps and shoulder harness, and then jumped down off the wing and waited for him to start the engine. Mark pressed and held the energizer switch, and listened to it winding up. When it reached its maximum speed, he moved it to the engage position and the big four-bladed propeller started turning. He moved the mixture to full rich and turned on the ignition switch, and the engine started to roar. He worked the throttle back and forth to keep it running. He gave the cockpit one more check, and then signaled for the sergeant to remove the chocks from in front of the wheels.

Mark taxied out to take-off position and scanned the sky. When he was satisfied that there were no other airplanes in the vicinity, he pushed the throttle to full power and took off.

The front lines were only thirty miles to the east of their base, and he had been cautioned not to get too close to them.

Mark started flying around the French countryside, making mental notes of prominent landmarks, such as rivers, hills, roads, railroad tracks, and an occasional prominent building or monument. It was pleasant to be able to fly as he wished, and he enjoyed looking at the predominantly farming countryside below. It was hard to believe that only thirty miles away, a violent war was going on, with people being maimed and killed. As he looked out of his canopy while banking around a village, a river, or a forest, he referred to his map and noted places that he had read or heard about before, places of bitter battles, not only in this war but in World War I as well: such as Bar-le-Duc, Marne, and Verdun.

Mark had been flying for about two hours, and decided he had better turn back to his field at Saint Dizier and prepare to land. In the States, he would normally call the tower and ask for landing instructions, but now, in combat, he had been told to maintain radio silence as much as possible, so as not to let the enemy know what was happening on our side of the lines. They were only to use the radios in case of emergencies.

Mark spotted the base and set up his traffic pattern to come in for his landing. As he entered the final approach, with the runway lining up in front of him, the mobile control tower shot off a red flare across his nose, signaling danger. Mark broke off his landing approach and pulled the airplane up into a climb.

"What's the trouble?" he asked the tower over his radio.

"You only have one landing gear down."

Mark looked around the cockpit and could see nothing unusual. All instruments were "in the green," and the hydraulic pressure which actuated the landing gear read a thousand pounds per square inch, which was normal.

He turned onto the downwind leg and said, "I'll recycle my gear and buzz you so that you can have a better look."

The control tower said "Okay."

Mark raised and lowered the gear handle, and then glanced at the hydraulic pressure again. It was still indicating normal. He turned back onto his final approach, but this time, aimed for the mobile control tower, which was located halfway down the runway, and just off to the right side. He was now down to about fifty feet off the ground, and just before passing alongside of the tower, turned on his side as he flew by them so they could get a good look at his underside.

"Nope! You still only have one gear down."

Mark started to climb again, wondering what to do. He told them that he would go up and try to shake the other one down. When he reached two thousand feet, he recycled the gear, this time rocking the wings violently. He then put the plane into a steep dive and made a high "g" pullout.

He also decided to try to increase the hydraulic pressure manually, to try to force the gear down. He clamped the control stick between his knees and reached over with both hands, grabbing the hydraulic pump handle near the floor to the left side of his seat and pumped it back and forth. He watched the pressure gauge build up. 1100—1200—1300—1400—1500 psi, red line! It was now sitting on the highest pressure the hydraulic lines could take without bursting. He then headed back for the tower and made another pass.

"Nope, still only one gear down."

Landing on one landing gear was almost certain to end in a fatal disaster. The plane would probably flip over, and go into a cartwheel at high speed. Gasoline lines would rupture spilling fuel over hot engine parts, with the plane ending up in a ball of fire.

Mark pulled up again, thinking this was a heck of a way to die. Here I am in combat, and haven't even had one shot fired at me in anger, yet I might get killed trying to get this bird onto the runway.

He continued flying downwind, and told the tower he would try to raise the other gear and fly by so that they could check to see if it came up. He moved the gear handle to the up position and buzzed the tower one more time.

"Yep! They're both up!"

As he pulled up into a climb, they asked, "What do you want to do? Belly in or bail out?"

Mark was a little disturbed at the thought of doing either and told them that he wanted to think about it. He still had a bit of extra fuel that he wanted to burn off to reduce the fire hazard, in case he finally decided to belly in. He also wanted to think through the bail-out procedures before taking that option.

There were two different ways he could bail out of a fighter.

He could trim up the airplane as best as he could for a straight and level flight. Then, open the canopy and climb out on the wing, while reaching over holding the stick trying to keep the airplane straight and level. He would also need to hold on tightly with the other hand so as not to be blown off the wing while he was doing so. Then he would let go of the stick and attempt to lie down and slide off the wing, hoping the tail didn't hit him as it went whizzing by. Finally, he would count to five to make sure he was well clear of the plane, and then pull the rip cord, hoping that the parachute would open without getting tangled. Pilots were not issued spare chutes, so everything had to be perfect the first time.

Or he could belly in, with all the unknowns of being in an aluminum-and-steel box laced with fuel and oil, sliding down concrete runway at about eighty miles an hour. For some reason the thought of staying with the airplane felt more comfortable to him. Parachuting seemed to have an awful lot of unknowns.

Mark pushed the mike button and told the tower: "I've decided to belly in."

Fully expecting them to be concerned for his safety, he was startled by their reply.

"Well, don't do it on the runway. We have a squadron returning from a mission in a few minutes, and we don't want to clutter up the runway."

Mark felt like he had been punched in the stomach! He suddenly felt very alone, and uncared for. However, this was combat, and he realized that the capability of the squadron to continue to perform its missions prevailed over any individual concerns.

Mark looked down at the field and tried to pick out a place that looked suitable for bellying in. At that time of the year in France, with the great amount of melting snow, and rain which was almost a daily occurrence, anything that wasn't paved was a sea of mud.

Mark radioed again. "Is it okay if I belly in alongside the runway, just to the left of it?"

"Yeah, that'll be okay," was the curt reply.

Mark set up a regular traffic pattern: downwind leg, base leg, and the turn onto final approach. He opened the canopy and stored all loose items. He locked his shoulder harness and, as he cleared the fence, turned off all switches and made his flair for a three-point attitude, waiting for the plane to hit the ground.

It would have been a perfect three-point landing if his wheels had been down, but with his wheels up, the minute the tail hit the ground, the nose flopped down, and the big air scoop of the engine nacelle started scooping up mud as he skidded across the field. He could feel the plane trying to nose over, and was holding his breath hoping that it wouldn't, because it would surely burst into flames if it did.

He felt like he was riding a wild, bucking bronco. As the plane finally started slowing down, he realized that he was going to make it. Now his only problem was getting out and as far away from it as he could in case it exploded.

He unfastened his shoulder harness as the plane was sliding to a stop, then jumped out of it and started running as fast as he could across the muddy field, trying to get away from it. He began to realize that he was being followed by an ambulance, and a doctor in a jeep. When he finally felt that he was safely far enough away from the plane, he stopped and turned to look back at it. The ambulance and jeep caught up with him. The doctor came running over and asked if he was hurt.

Mark felt himself and looked down at his hands, and said, "No, it doesn't look like it."

"Are you sure?" he said. "If you're cut at all, I could give you the Purple Heart."

Mark checked again and said, "Nope, I'm okay."

He was given a ride back to the officers' shack, and felt awful about wrecking one of the squadron's planes the first time he took it up. These guys are going to think I'm a real 8-ball. He didn't believe the accident was anything that he could have prevented, but it still worried him. Was there anything else that I could have done? He wondered. But he couldn't think of anything.

The answer came later in the afternoon when the crew chief raised the plane on a hoist in the hangar and found the problem. A round metal bar, called the shrink strut, was designed to compress the shock absorber as the wheels came up, so that they would fit into the wing's wheel well. Apparently, the metal bar in the right wheel well broke due to metal fatigue while it was retracted. The wheel was wedged so tightly that nothing on earth could have shaken it down.

Mark felt relieved when he heard one of the pilots say, "That plane has always been a dog anyway. Good riddance."

CHAPTER 22

(France)

Mail call is one of the most important things that a soldier eagerly looks forward to every day. It is his only communication with his family and loved ones back home. Mark was thrilled when he got his first letter from Joanne:

Mark darling,

The news on the radio this past week has been very worrying. I hope you are well and stay well. I can't wait to get you home.

As I type this tonight, I pause to look down at my pretty little ring and think of the time you surprised me with it that night at Cleaver's Farm road. I love and treasure it.

Love, Joanne

* * * *

After his first mission in which he failed to hit the targeted railroad yard, Marks accuracy improved considerably, and now he could hit just about anything he went after.

Their main task was supporting the ground troops of General Patton's Third Army. It consisted mainly of strafing and dive-bombing targets in front of them such as tanks, trucks, troops and trains. They would also protect them from air attacks by intercepting enemy aircraft whenever they appeared. During the next thirty days, Mark flew sixteen missions, and the squadron lost five pilots.

The squadron had a policy that if a pilot survived thirty days of combat, he was given a jeep and was permitted to go to Paris for three days. Mark and Bill Carlson, with whom he had become good friends, climbed into their assigned jeep and headed to Paris together.

The ride took them through small villages along the way. Most of the villages they saw had suffered varying degrees of battle damage. The road had also been bombed in places, requiring slight detours around the craters.

Upon entering Paris, they drove into the heart of the city, up the Place de la Concorde and the Rue Madeleine, to a hotel near the Opera House.

Bill parked the jeep in front of the hotel, raised the hood, pulled off the distributer rotor, and put it in his pocket. Jeeps didn't have keys, so it was a way to keep someone from driving off with theirs. The hotel was designated as transit officers' quarters, and was being run by Special Services for officers on leave. They checked in with the Red Cross worker at the desk. She gave them their keys and told them how to get to their room.

The room was nice with a large window and a small balcony facing the street. The nicest things in the room, however, were the two beds with clean white sheets and blankets. It was a welcome change to their rugged sleeping bags back at the base. They were only charged seventy-five cents a day for their room, since the hotel was considered to be an army barracks. Mark was sure that in peacetime it would cost at least a hundred dollars a day because of its prime location. After a short rest and a much-welcome shower, they headed into town.

Mark couldn't help but be impressed with the beauty of Paris: the trees and openness of the Place de la Concorde, the river Seine with its stone bridges, and the many statues and arches.

He remembered taking an art class in high school learning that the Louvre Art Museum was the greatest art gallery in the world. Even though he knew it was closed during the war, with all of its valuable paintings hidden away somewhere, he still wanted to at least see the outside of the Louvre.

Two young Frenchmen were walking toward them, and Mark stopped them to ask, in halting French, if they could direct him to the Louvre. After several attempts and a lot of hand waving, they got their message across, and the men motioned for Mark and Bill to follow them. One spoke a bit of English and attempted to carry on a conversation as they walked. Mark finally understood that he was trying to tell them he knew an American lady, a lieutenant, a nurse.

Mark asked him if he had dated her. The question seemed to puzzle him. He didn't seem to understand what was meant by the term "date." After a few moments he seemed to see the light, but when he said, "You mean did I seduce her?" Mark cringed and changed the subject.

As the four of them walked around the outside of the Louvre, Mark said, "The grounds around the museum are very nice but I'm a bit disappointed in the building itself. It seems rather stark to be housing such beautiful works of art as the Mona Lisa. I wonder if I'll be lucky enough to come back someday after the war and see the inside."

He and Bill thanked the fellows for their help and walked over to the stairs leading down to the metro. They looked at the map next to the stairwell, showing the subway routes and transfer points, and decided to go to Pigalle.

The French had a policy of not charging soldiers to ride the metro. However, the amount was so small that the army suggested they pay the fare, if they were so inclined. It would help the French economy. Most Americans usually did.

As they rode along, a rather well-dressed, older Frenchman sitting near them struck up a conversation. He spoke English rather well and asked where they were going. When they told him, he said, "You Americans are always going to Pigalle looking for the ladies, yes? There are better places."

He had piqued their interest, yet they had some reservations about becoming too involved with a stranger.

"Where do you suggest?" Bill asked.

"I'll show you."

After some hesitation, they left the metro with the stranger and walked a few blocks with him to a two-story house surrounded by a picket fence and a small garden. They entered the gate and climbed the stairs to the front porch. It could have been a nice home in the States, nested in an elegant but older neighborhood.

The stranger rang the bell. The door was opened by an attractive and exuberant, middle-aged woman. She greeted their newly acquired friend with a kiss on both cheeks, and motioned for them to come in. They entered a hallway and were shown into the parlor on their left. They sat on one of the sofas as the man and woman spoke in French at some length.

Finally, the man turned to them and said, "Madame says four of her girls went to the movies this afternoon and won't be back for at least another hour, and her other two girls are busy."

Well, that was that. They thanked him and boarded the metro again, bound for Pigalle.

They walked the length of the main street several times and finally sat down at a sidewalk café. Each ordered a glass of red wine. Sidewalk cafés seemed to be one of the great institutions of France. Mark found it amazing that a country with so few sunny days would have so many cafés where people could sit outside, have a drink, and watch the world go by. There seemed to be an unwritten law that once you ordered a drink, the waiters left you alone. They never pressured you to buy another, nor to leave. He believed he and Bill could have spent the entire day there undisturbed if they had wanted to.

They had been sitting taking in the scenery for about fifteen minutes when two girls turned into the café and sat at a table near them. It wasn't long before they struck up a conversation and joined the girls at their table. In spite of the language barrier, they managed to communicate fairly well. It seemed apparent that the girls were willing to go to their room with them, but there was one problem: they were not allowed to bring girls to their rooms in a military hotel. So they asked the girls if they knew of a place where they could get a room. "Oui. We know one."

Bill and Mark followed them down the street to a small, but very nice hotel located at the pointed end of a pie-shaped street. Their room was on the third floor, and they rode up to it in a caged lift that ascended on the inside of a circular staircase. Their room was also pie-shaped. The French doors at one end opened out onto a wrought iron balcony. They all stepped out to take in the panoramic view, and take a few deep breaths of the fresh autumn air.

The room had two good-sized beds, and it didn't take long to get into them—Bill and his girl in one, and Mark and his girl in the other. They turned out the lights and made love several times. It occurred to Mark that it would be fun to trade partners for a while, but he didn't have the nerve to bring it up, even though he suspected no one would have minded.

In the morning, they frolicked around in the room for a while. He asked the girls if he could take their pictures in the nude. They were not bashful. Without hesitation, they stood naked, arm in arm near the French doors where the daylight was best, and posed for him.

When they got back to the squadron, Mark found out that the pilot who flew his plane while he was gone was shot down and killed.

CHAPTER   23

(Germany)

"Browning Squadron, you've got 20 bandits at three o'clock, five miles and closing."

It was the voice of ground control announcing the image they had just spotted on their new piece of equipment, called 'radar.'

This would be Mark's first encounter with enemy fighters and he felt his pulse quickening and his muscles tightening. It would be his ultimate test as a pilot. Air-to-air combat!

The squadron was flying 12 airplanes, and was on its way to a German target when the call came.

He started to sweat. He squinted intently through his canopy in the three o'clock direction, but couldn't see anything but clear, blue sky.

The squadron continued silently toward their assigned target, waiting for an update on the position of the threatening Nazi fighters.

Ground control broke the silence again. "Browning Flight, you have twenty, repeat, twenty bandits, three o'clock, three miles and closing fast." He again desperately strained to see some sign of the planes coming toward them, but saw nothing.

There were only twelve of them and their planes were not considered to be as maneuverable, nor as fast, as the Messerschmitt ME-109 or the Focke-Wulf FW-190.

Damn it.

He wished that he was slightly far-sighted instead of slightly near-sighted. He had always been able to pass the eye exams for pilots, but it was easier for him to see nearer things than those at a distance.

Not a word was spoken by their squadron leader as they continued flying in complete silence, straight and level, toward their assigned target.

Ground control had just finished the last message, ". . . one mile and closing," when someone spotted them.

"Here they come!" was no sooner shouted than the flight of twenty ME-109s roared through their formation, firing their 20 mm cannons, which shot through the noses of their planes. They shot down two P-47s as they passed and then scattered as they started to climb.

Mark got a glimpse of one of the struck Thunderbolts as it spun out of sight.

Major Adams sprung to life. "Browning Flight, jettison bombs. Let's go get 'em!"

American tactics were for pilots to stay with their element leaders. So as they started their chase, there were two P-47s chasing one ME-109. It made a combination that was very hard to get away from.

The ME-109 in front of them went into a climb, and Lt Martin, with Mark as his wing man, started climbing after him. The Messerschmitt was climbing slightly steeper than they were, but they were managing to stay fairly close to him without stalling.

Mark was flying to the right and slightly below his element leader, and could see the ME-109 by looking up through the top of his canopy. If he could only pull up a bit, he could get his sights on it. But he was already approaching a stall and dared not pull up any more.

It was a crazy idea, but he thought it would be a shame to get into air-to-air combat and yet never fire a shot at the enemy. So even though he knew he wasn't pointing anywhere near the plane, he squeezed off a burst.

What he hadn't counted on was the recoil from the eight, 50-caliber machine guns. He was flying so close to a stall that the guns stalled him momentarily. He popped the stick forward enough to regain flying speed. Luckily, he had only lost a few feet in the process. He was again flying next to his element leader and watching the ME-109 out of the top of his canopy.

Amazingly, the ME-109 didn't seem to be able to out climb them. Then he remembered that their P-47 was one of the few airplanes that had a turbo supercharger, and it helped them maintain their performance at higher altitudes. The ME-109 did not have one, and its performance was dropping off dramatically as it climbed into thinner air.

Suddenly the German fighter did a strange thing. It stopped climbing, flipped over, and went into a shallow dive.

What in the world is he doing? Mark wondered. Why had he flipped? Could it be that he stalled out?

Lt. Martin and Mark quickly took up the chase. It now became apparent that he was trying to dive to a nearby cloud to get away.

Lt. Martin was now in hot pursuit, and started firing. Mark could see the puffs from his guns as they fired. He looked at the ME-109, trying to see where the bullets were landing but couldn't see signs of any hits. His leader fired another burst, and he fully expected the ME-109 to catch fire or explode. Eight, 50-caliber machine guns were a lot of fire power to bear on one target. Yet nothing happened. He saw no signs of any bullets hitting the plane.

What was wrong? Mark wondered. His element leader was an experienced pilot, and surely well qualified in air-to-air gunnery.

Look, he thought, if you can't hit him, get out of the way so that I can have a go at him.

Meanwhile, the German was getting closer to the cloud and if he made it in, they would lose him.

Mark then watched as his leader did a wing-over and raked through him with a burst as he pulled down diagonally, passing very close behind him. At last there were some hits. He could see several sparks and a small explosion near the engine as his leader pulled away. For the first time, Mark had a clear, unobstructed view of the ME-109 and was surprised to see that he seemed to be flying intact, and was still headed for the cloud.

Mark brought his gun sight on him and pulled through with what he estimated to be the proper lead for the situation. He squeezed the trigger but was disappointed to see that he did not hit him. He tried another burst. Still no hits. He remembered from gunnery training that the normal tendency was not to lead the target enough; so he increased the lead and fired again. Still no hits. He raked the guns back and forth across the plane, using his rudder pedals. Still no hits! What was wrong? He had done very well in air-to-air gunnery back in the States. Why couldn't he hit him?

A shudder suddenly went through Mark. He had been concentrating so intently on trying to shoot the Nazi down, that he didn't realized how fast he was going nor how close to him he had gotten. He had to desperately swerve to keep from flying into him. In fact, he was now starting to pass him! Apparently the German had chopped his throttle and was slowing down considerably.

A frightening thought suddenly struck Mark. He was about to slide past him and become the pursued, instead of the pursuer. He had to slow down, and slow down fast. He chopped the throttle, and did everything possible to increase his drag. First and most effectively, he quickly lowered the landing gear. Never mind that he was flying about a hundred miles an hour over the speed at which they were supposed to be lowered. The plane shuttered.

It was slow down now or die, might as well die trying.
He needed to slow down more.

He lowered the flaps, even though at his speed they might be blown off or get bent.

Thankfully, they held.

So far so good, Mark thought. The only trick left was to open the engine cowl flaps. He did it, then held his breath and waited.

He was now alongside of the ME-109, and could see the pilot in the cockpit. He was shaking his fist at him.

Mark was still sliding slowly alongside of him and was starting to pass him, but he could feel the drag of his gear and flaps slowing him down considerably. At last he ceased gaining on him, and they were now flying at about the same speed, side by side. He gradually began to feel his plane slow down and start sliding back.

As he cleared the tail of the German's plane, he flipped up into a 90° bank and started firing as he pulled through behind him. He got several hits, and the ME-109 immediately started smoking and caught fire. As Mark pulled away, he could see him dropping into a flaming, spiraling dive.

Mark looked around for his flight leader and the rest of his squadron. There was no one in sight! More frightening was the fact that he knew there were still about nineteen enemy aircraft in the area, and he was alone. Even worse, he didn't even know where he was.

He thought back to the morning's briefing. Their target was somewhere near Trier on the Moselle River, but in the heat of the dogfight he had lost his bearing. He was now flying over the cloud layer that the German pilot had been trying to reach, and could not see the land below. He thought maybe the rest of the squadron might be below the overcast and decided to make an instrument let-down through it.

Even that was unnerving because he seldom had the chance to practice instrument flying. He also didn't know how thick the overcast was. It might extend so low that it would be dangerously close to the ground. He decided to take a chance, and he concentrated on his instruments as he entered the clouds and maintained a shallow dive. Luckily, the overcast was only a few thousand feet thick, and he broke out to see the German landscape below, dominated by a large river, apparently the Moselle.

Suddenly he got a glimpse of an airplane flying in a steep bank and noticed something very strange about it. It looked like it had static electricity dancing along its wings. He immediately realized that it was a Focke-Wulf 190 turning toward him, and what looked like static electricity were the muzzles of his guns firing at him.

Mark whipped his airplane into a steep turn toward him and started firing back. The two planes passed each other with their guns blazing away, narrowly missing a high speed, head-on collision. Somehow they failed to get any hits on each other and, as the Focke-Wulf went by, Mark pulled into a steep turn in order to engage him again. But as he watched, the Nazi pulled up into the overcast and was gone.

As if having nineteen enemy planes in the area and being lost from his squadron were not enough problems, he was now beginning to get low on fuel and was not sure how to get back to the base. He decided to fly south, parallel to the river.

He continued to scan the sky in search of other planes.

As he looked upward during one of his scans, he witnessed a sight that was both beautiful and frightening. There was his squadron in one big Luffberry circle, trying to get on the tail of some of the German fighters, who in turn were trying to get on the tails of the Americans. He immediately started climbing to join them. As he drew nearer, he heard his commander say, "Okay Browning Flight, let's break off and go home."

As they turned out of the circle and headed west, Mark caught up with them and slid into the formation.

When they got back to the base and took tally, they learned that the squadron had lost two planes and had shot down six of the enemy's.

Mark kept wondering why he and his element leader had such a hard time hitting the German plane when it was right in front of them, and concluded that the pilot was flying in a skid. By pressing the left rudder in and turning the stick to the right, the airplane would point slightly to the right and appear to be flying in that direction, but would actually be sliding straight ahead. It was a very subtle and clever maneuver, and he wondered why they were never taught it. The pilot was obviously very experienced and probably an ace.

CHAPTER 24

(Saint Dizier, France)

John Cool, who was a contractor in civilian life, was talking to a group in the officers' shack one day. He said, "If I can get some lumber and some of you pilots together to pitch in, I could make our shack here twice the size and it would be more comfortable for all of us."

It was a great offer, and rumor had it that there were the remains of a former German army base about five miles away. Although most of the buildings were destroyed, there was still a lot of good lumber just lying around to be had.

Five pilots volunteered to go over with John to get the lumber. Mark and Bill were two of them. They were driven to the area in two GI trucks by enlisted men who were their regular drivers.

It was early December and the weather was below freezing. They all wore their fleece-lined jackets over their uniforms and gloves.

The rumor proved to be true. As they drove into the former courtyard, they saw lots of good boards scattered around the frozen ground. Some were still nailed together and had to be hammered apart.

After a couple hours, it started getting dark, and the driver of Mark's truck said, "Sir, I've got to get back to the base or I'll miss chow."

"Okay, Sarge, you can go back with the other truck. It's just getting ready to leave. Lt. Carlson and I will drive this one back as soon as we finish loading up another stack of good boards."

Fifteen minutes later they were ready to go back, and Mark looked up at the truck and asked, "Bill, have you ever driven a G truck?"

"No I haven't, have you?"

"No, but I'll give it a try."

Mark climbed into the driver's seat and Bill got in beside him. The ground had been mud in warmer days, and previous trucks had made some deep ruts in it as they drove through with their heavy cargos. The ground was now frozen hard.

As Mark started driving across the icy field, he felt their front wheels fall into one of the frozen ruts and the truck rested on its front differential. The front wheels now spun freely in the rut and could not get enough traction to move the truck. Bill got out and tried to pry some boards under the wheels without success.

Two French boys, who had been watching them, witnessed their plight. One came up to Mark and said, "chevals?" Mark remembered from his high school French class that chevals means horses. So he answered, "chevals, oui." The boys then disappeared over the hill.

Mark and Bill struggled with the truck for another 20 minutes, and were surprised when they heard the sound of cow bells coming over the hill. It was an unbelievable sight. The boys' father appeared leading a pair of oxen that had bells on their collars. Mark had always heard that oxen were strong, so he felt their troubles were over.

The farmer hooked up the oxen to the back of the truck and yelled a command in French for them to pull. They yanked with very little effort but the truck didn't budge. The farmer then took the pitchfork he was holding and jabbed the rear of one of the oxen as he yelled a command. The beast let out a loud moan and lunged forward, while the other one stood still. He then went over and jabbed the other ox. When it surged forward the first one stood still. After a couple of these episodes without the truck moving an inch, he disconnected the oxen, disappeared back over the hill, and never returned.

Mark and Bill were now beginning to get worried. It was well below freezing, and starting to get dark. They could be stranded here all night. They got out of the truck and were starting to work again, trying to get some wood wedged under the tires, when they heard the sound of a jeep coming down the narrow dirt road next to the field. Bill rushed out to flag it down before it could go past them. The GI driving the jeep said, "I can't help you, but there is a truck behind me that may be able to help."

They eagerly looked for it to appear and got it to stop as it reached the clearing. Mark was happy to see the winch on its front bumper. After explaining their plight to the sergeant who was driving, he aligned his truck about 10 yards behind theirs, fastened the winch to their rear bumper and turned on the motor.

The cable strained but, to their shock, their truck stayed still and the truck with the winch slid forward over the icy ground. They were flabbergasted. This was their last hope and it wasn't working.

The sergeant surprised them by backing his truck up to a nearby tree and tying the truck to it with a strong rope. When he turned on the motor again, the rope strained, the truck strained, the tree strained, and the cable strained. Then there was one loud shudder as the stuck truck bounced out of the rut. The truck was free! They thanked the sergeant for his help and got back into their newly freed truck. Mark started it up, put it in first gear and drove it out onto a paved road. Unfortunately, he was not able to get it into second gear. He knew there was something called "double clutching," but neither he nor Bill knew how to do it. So they ended up driving all the way back to their base in first gear.

John Cool, true to his word, did build the addition to their shack and made it much more useful.

CHAPTER 25

(Saint Dizier, France)

The squadron adopted a small French bar in the nearby town of St. Dizier. It was a place to go in their off time, drink a few beers, and exchange stories of their encounters.

Many of the pilots had been in the squadron longer than Mark. Some were even involved in the eventful D-Day landing of US troops in Normandy. Mark was fascinated by the story that Henry Wicker was telling.

"A few days after our troops landed on the French coast, the squadron started flying off of a hastily-made, temporary airstrip near St. Lo.

"I was one of a flight of four flying our first mission from the coast of France. We were ordered to bomb and strafe a German ammunition dump located about halfway to Paris. It would be a long flight over unfamiliar territory. Navigation would be a challenge.

"We found the arsenal and destroyed it with spectacular results. As we were heading home, we were having trouble finding our small airstrip. It blended in among all the turmoil that was occurring with the army troops on the ground. The situation was beginning to get desperate.

"Our flight leader, Paul Bishop, spotted an empty air field and we lost no time landing on it.

"As we taxied trying to find a parking area, we noticed a lot of wires sticking out of the ground with cloth streamers attached to them. We carefully steered around them, assuming that they marked where land mines were buried.

"We pulled to a stop in a clear area, and looked around at what seemed to be an abandoned field.

"A farmer came running across his pasture, waving his arms excitedly and shouted something to us in French. One of the pilots, Andy La Roc, was of French Canadian descent and understood him. 'He is saying this is a German air field. The planes are gone, but some people are still hiding behind the hangars. He wants us to take off and strafe behind them.'

"Paul made a quick decision to perform the famous military maneuver known as 'Let's get the hell out of here.'

"We climbed back into our planes and immediately took off.

"But as we started climbing, my plane ran out of fuel. I bellied in on a farmer's field and slid to a stop. As I was unstrapping myself, a farmer came running out of the woods, rushed up to my plane, and signaled for me to quickly follow him. I lost no time jumping out of the plane and ran with the farmer back into the woods. When we reached his house, I learned that he was a member of the French underground. They blew up bridges and created havoc for the Germans wherever they could. They welcomed an American pilot into their fold and, since I was an officer, they wanted me to lead them.

"I had no idea how to go about blowing up bridges, but immediately found myself doing just that. Three days later the group was captured, and we were scheduled to be shot by a firing squad the following morning. We were held prisoner overnight in the court house in the center of a small town.

"When morning came, I watched out my window as the first four of our group were marched out into the courtyard, lined up, and shot by a four-man firing squad.

"I nervously kept watching as the bodies were being dragged away and the next four were marched out. I broke out into a nervous sweat as I realized that I would be in the next group of four to be killed.

"The second group of four was shot.

"As soon as the dead bodies were taken away, I would be with the last three in our group to be executed.

"We were marched out and lined up with our hands tied up behind us

The German officer lined up his squad, preparing to give the command to fire. I knew I just had a few more moments to live.

"As I stood there leaning forward, my dog tags swung out from under my shirt. Out of desperation, I shouted, 'I am an American officer!'

"The head of the firing squad paused and looked at me, and, in broken English, asked me what I said.

"I said, 'I am an American officer, see my dog tags?'

"The German clutched them in his hands, looked at them, pulled me out of the line up, and shot the others.

"The great sense of relief at being spared the killing rain of bullets penetrating my body was indescribable. I felt thankful for my good fortune, yet depressed at the fate of the men I had gotten to know and respect for their daring efforts to save their country.

"There was so much turmoil in the area the next few days that I was able to escape and find my way back to my squadron."

CHAPTER 26

(France)

Mark was enjoying the extra room in the officers' shack now that John Cool, with the help of some of the pilots, had successfully enlarged it. The lumber that they recovered from the nearby abandoned German base was enough to complete the job. The weather was freezing outside but Mark found space near the potbellied stove to sit and write a letter to Joanne. She was still faithfully writing to him three times a week, and he loved her for that.

He had just gotten one from her that morning and started writing one in return.

My Darling,

I've just received your wonderful letter today, and wonder how I can find the words to tell you how good it makes me feel. My words seem so inadequate, so I'm going to borrow a few from Elizabeth Barrett Browning.

How do I love thee? Let me count the ways. I love thee to the depth my soul can reach. I love thee with the breath, smiles, and tears, of all my life, and if God choose, I shall but love thee better after death.

With all my love, Mark

Mark had now flown and survived another ten missions, so he and Bill got to go back to Paris for three days.

It was getting near enough to Christmas that Mark decided to see if he could do some Christmas shopping. It would be nice to buy Joanne a pair of black lace panties and brassiere, he thought. they would especially be a bit risqué coming from Paris.

When they checked into their hotel, Mark noticed a sign on the bulletin board in the lobby next to the desk. If anyone needed help doing their Christmas shopping, there were French women volunteers available to help them. It sounded like a good idea, so he requested the service from the Red Cross lady at the desk. She made a few phone calls and finally told him that he was in luck; the Countess was free and would meet him in the lobby in thirty minutes.

The Countess turned out to be an attractive lady, about thirty-five years old, but very businesslike. She led him over to a glassed-in room, just off the lobby, and indicated that they should sit down for a few minutes and talk.

"Do you have any American dollars?" she asked.

He was taken a bit by surprise with her question, since selling American dollars was illegal, although most of the soldiers did it occasionally because they could usually get much better rates than the official rate. However, he had not expected to hear it coming from a Countess.

"All I have is a five dollar bill," he said, but she seemed pleased to buy even that.

"Now," she said, "what is it you want to buy?"

Slightly embarrassed, he told her about the black lace lingerie he had in mind.

"Oh," she said, "you don't want to buy those in Paris. They are very expensive."

"How much?"

"About ninety dollars."

"Then what do you have in mind?" he asked.

"I know of a little shop that has beautiful, hand-painted handkerchiefs. They make wonderful gifts!"

He couldn't think of anything he would rather not have than hand-painted handkerchiefs, but at her insistence, they walked a few blocks to a small shop. The moment they walked in, she was greeted warmly by the proprietor. They hugged and kissed, and it seemed clear that if they were not relatives, they were at least very old friends.

Mark was shown several trays of handkerchiefs, and somehow ended up leaving the shop with three handkerchiefs which cost him about thirty-eight dollars.

"Now we go to a perfume shop and buy some nice perfume," the Countess said. This did not excite him either.

Was he being had? If so, he seemed to be unable or unwilling to do anything about it. And soon, after another scene of kissing and hugging with another proprietor, he had bought fifty-five dollars' worth of perfume.

So the end result of his shopping trip with the Countess was that he had spent almost a hundred dollars on things he did not want. He felt he could have bought the black lace lingerie probably for less money, if he hadn't had so much help.

CHAPTER 27

France)

The Germans suddenly pulled a surprisingly strong counter-attack during December 1944, pushing through the front lines with their Panzer tanks, and trying to drive a bulge between the Allied troops in the north and those in the south of Europe. It was a fierce charge with almost a million men involved and thousands of casualties, and came to be known as the Battle of the Bulge.

The southern portion of their thrust was within twenty-five miles of Mark's airfield, and he was in constant fear that some of the Nazi troops might infiltrate their base and blow up their aircraft during the night. Mark was particularly worried about being shot in his sleeping bag. He could visualize waking up some night and staring into the barrel of his own pistol pointed at him just before some German pulled the trigger. The thought often made it difficult for him to sleep soundly.

The advancing German army had surrounded an American battalion at the town of Bastogne, Belgium. An airborne division under the command of General McAuliffe went to aid the beleaguered troops and also became surrounded by the Germans. When asked to surrender, General McAuliffe sent back his famous reply, "Nuts," which was interpreted as, "Go to hell."

The weather was bad that time of year, and it grounded Mark's squadron quite often. He did manage to go on a raid dive-bombing a fuel dump, which burned spectacularly. He also strafed some trains loaded with liquid oxygen which were destined to be used in the V-2 rockets. When these hit, they produced extremely violent explosions with strong shock waves emanating from them.

Their combat films showed train wheels and axles flying up, just missing their airplanes. During such low-altitude work, there was always a danger of flying into the debris of the explosion.

CHAPTER 28

(France)

Whenever the squadron left for a mission, four airplanes and their pilots always stayed behind to defend the field in case of an attack by the enemy.

One freezing day in late December, Mark and three other pilots sat in a tent near the end of the runway pulling this duty, which was known as "runway alert."

The tent had a small, makeshift table, two benches, and a field phone hanging from the tent pole.

It was a miserable and boring job which everyone hated. No one had ever received a call to scramble. They just sat out there freezing for three or four hours, trying to play cards to pass the time away while waiting for the squadron to return.

Every half hour, they had to run out through the snow, climb up into their airplanes, and run up the engines for five minutes. That kept them prepared for an immediate take-off, if one was required.

It was the day after Christmas, and their runway alert was proceeding just as it always did, with time hanging heavy on their hands.

Suddenly, the silence was broken by the ringing of the field phone.

They looked at each other in disbelief. Mark picked it up and listened as the voice from Command and Control Center gave out instructions.

"Browning Alert, take off immediately. Call ground control when airborne for further instructions."

The four pilots ran out to their airplanes and took off. As they started climbing, Mark reported back to ground control. "Ground control, Browning Alert is airborne and climbing. Over."

"Roger, Browning. Turn to a heading of 303 and fly to the town of Reims, then report for further instructions. Over."

As they reached Reims at 25,000 feet, Mark called.

"Ground control, this is Browning Flight circling Reims. Over."

"Roger, Browning. Your mission is to escort a flight of C-47 transports into Bastogne. They will be going in to drop desperately-needed supplies to the ground troops that are surrounded there. Over."

"Roger, wilco."

They started their circling, and wondered if they would engage any enemy fighters.

In a few minutes, ground control again broke the silence. "Browning Flight, you may expect heavy enemy interception on this flight. Repeat. You may expect heavy interception—up to one hundred enemy aircraft."

One hundred enemy aircraft! Mark couldn't believe his ears!

There were four of them, and they were going to defend the transports against a hundred ME-109s and Focke-Wulfs! This is it, Mark thought, this is my last mission. No way can each of us handle twenty-five bandits. I'm good for one, maybe two if I'm lucky, but that will be it.

None of the four of them said a word, but they were all thinking the same thing.

It was a strange new tactic that the Germans were using. With their dwindling fuel supply, they flew very few small, individual missions. Instead, they saved up fuel for an occasional big strike, knocking out several airfields at once or, in this case, supporting the Panzer tanks in their drive to the North Sea.

The sky had cleared, and the visibility was good. It would only take fifteen minutes more to reach Bastogne from where they were. Mark kept scanning his instruments to make sure his plane was in tip-top condition for the fight of its life.

The voice of doom then came back through the head-phones once again. "Browning Flight, the cargo planes are on the way. Repeat, you may expect very heavy enemy interception, up to a hundred and twenty ME-109s."

Ground control had apparently spotted twenty more planes.

It was getting worse by the minute!

Another problem was beginning to arise: fuel.

If he had to fight, he wanted to have enough fuel. Violent throttle changes and the use of water injection to increase power consumed fuel at a high rate.

Where were those C-47s? Come on; let's get this thing over with! Mark thought.

As they circled silently for another ten minutes, Mark wondered if he would get shot down immediately, or if he would be able to shoot down some of them before he went.

Finally, the ground controller came through with the mes-sage that would let them live to fight another day: "Browning Flight, your mission is scrubbed. Return to base."

It was a great load lifted from their shoulders, but later the pilots would always wonder what it would have been like to dog-fight more than a hundred airplanes.

The decision to cancel the mission turned out to be a very wise one. Because the Germans would have to land their big armada of fighters soon, their shortage of fuel would prohibit them from sending up another large group of planes anytime soon.

The C-47s would only have to wait an hour more, and then fly in practically unchallenged.

CHAPTER 29

(France; Belgium)

The letters from Joanne were becoming fewer and farther apart. Mark was starting to believe that his greatest fear was finally happening. She had met someone else at the USO dance, and fallen in love with him. After all, with the many healthy, handsome young cadets drooling over her every weekend, and with him being completely out of sight and reach…what could he expect?

Mark tried not to dwell on it, but the thought of her kept returning to his mind.

* * * *

The Allied armies were now regrouping for their final push into Germany. The Allied command, headed by General Eisenhower, determined that the main thrust would be to reach the Rhine River, and then into the northern part of Germany. As a result, some of the squadrons which had been supporting General Patton, who was fighting in the central portion of Germany, were being taken away from him and moved to support General Hodges's First Army in the north.

Mark's squadron was one of the groups to be moved, and they were being sent to a base in Belgium.

When moving day came, all the non-flying personnel, including the enlisted ground crew, mechanics, cooks, administrative personnel, and non-flying officers such as the executive officer, doctor, and armament officer, broke camp, loaded all the movable equipment into trucks, and drove in a convoy up to the new base.

The fighter pilots were to take off from the old base a Saint Dizier in France, fly a mission into Germany, and then land at their new airstrip in Belgium. Their mission was to bomb some factories in the Ruhr area of Germany. It was the center o Germany's manufacturing activity, and the most heavily defended area in the world.

As they entered the Ruhr, all hell broke loose. It was by fa the worst barrage of antiaircraft fire they had ever experienced Almost immediately, one of their planes took a direct hit by an "88" and disintegrated. They circled some factories on the Rhine and got some good direct hits. Mark's dive-bombing had improved considerably since his first mission, and he was able to get several good hits on factories and storage buildings.

Dive-bombing was really an art rather than a science in the Thunderbolt. Because of the large engine, the gun sight could no be moved to a low enough angle that would allow the ring and do to be placed on the target. If they did place the sight on the target and released the bombs, they would always hit the ground consid erably short of the target. To avoid this happening, their dive bombing technique was to roll over, go into a dive, put the gun sight on the target, then pull through until the target disappeared below the nose. Then, when they got "that funny feeling," they would release the bomb. A good dive-bomb pilot was one who had calibrated his funny feeling just right.

As they approached their new base, Mark was startled to see some very large piles of slag scattered around. They were the byproduct of the local coal mines. The piles were several hundred feet high, and would be something he would have to reckon with if they flew back from a mission at a low altitude, trying to stay under the clouds.

As they circled the new airstrip, Mark noticed that the run way was made of interlocking pierced planks of sheet metal laid down on a farmer's field. He also noticed that there wasn't a hangar or any other building in sight.

They made their usual "tactical approach" and landed on the rough runway. Mark taxied over to one of the spots left in the parking area, opened the canopy, and was hit in the face by a blast of ice cold air. It was freezing there.

Sergeant Newton, his crew chief, climbed up on to the wing and greeted him. Even though they had just left each other a few hours earlier, it was nice to see a familiar face at the new base. As he helped to unstrap Mark, he said, "Congratulations, sir. You've been promoted to 1st Lieutenant." Needless to say, Mark was thrilled at the news. It was especially welcome after what had been a long, hard day.

But the worst was yet to come. As he climbed out of the plane, he asked Sgt. Newton where the pilots were supposed to go. He was freezing and really needed a place to get warm.

"There is no place, sir," he answered. "The only thing here is this runway, and the open fields partly covered with snow. They're trying to put up a Quonset hut, but that probably won't be up til tomorrow."

Mark jumped down off the wing and looked around at the bleak fields surrounding their planes. He went over and joined some of the other pilots who were standing around thrashing their arms, trying to keep warm. He wondered how long they could stand the bitter cold without a fire of some sort. The only sign of heat was coming from a little chimney sticking out of what appeared to be a small gypsy trailer down at one end of the field. He was informed that it was their commanding officer's trailer. It was found somewhere in France and had been brought up in the convoy for him.

They noticed pieces of a Quonset hut lying on the ground in several piles, and would have gladly pitched in to help build it, but they were told that there were some parts missing.

They stood around in the cold for almost an hour until they couldn't stand it any longer and decided to go over and knock on the door of the commanding officer's trailer. They were let in by some pilots who had already crowded in before them. The CO was sitting at a small table in a corner. He seemed to understand the situation and tolerated the crowding. He told them that the executive officer was in town trying to find some quarters for them, and that they all would just have to do the best they could until he returned.

What seemed like an eternity later, a truck pulling a small covered trailer arrived. They all piled in wherever they could find room, and were driven to a school house in the center of the tiny Belgium town a few miles from their field. Cots and bedrolls were delivered by trucks and set up on the floor of the gymnasium. Thankfully, their B-4 bags were also on the truck.

CHAPTER 30

(Belgium)

Boxes of K-rations were passed out, and Mark was lucky. His contained a can of corned beef.

He slept rather well in the large, cold room filled with cots arranged somewhat helter-skelter.

When Mark awoke in the morning, it took him a few seconds to get his bearings and remember where he was. He was surprised to see several Belgian children wandering around between the cots talking to the pilots. One of the boys noticed that he had awaken and walked over to him. He asked in broken English if Mark had any dirty clothes that his mother could wash for him. He thought for a minute, trying to make out the significance of what the lad was saying, and then it hit him. Yes, you bet. He would be happy for the opportunity to have his dirty clothes laundered. Normally he had to do it himself, and always put it off til the last minute. As he gathered the dirty clothing out of his B-4 bag, the boy explained that Mark would have to provide the soap, a request which he could readily understand since there was an acute shortage of soap in Europe. Soap was no problem for him, because the pilots all got soap in their PX rations every few weeks. Mark had no idea how much they would be charged for the laundering, nor did he much care. He, like the other men, was just glad to be getting it done.

The toilets at the school house turned out to be something else. They were all lined up out in the middle of the school yard, out in the open, with no walls, no doors, and no privacy, and partly covered with snow. Apparently, boys and girls alike used them, and there did not seem to be any pretense of modesty.

CHAPTER 31

Belgium)

After a quick K-ration breakfast, the pilots were driven out o the airstrip to take off on their first mission from their new base. Mark was surprised to see that the planes were very heavily oaded that morning, with a 1,000-pound bomb hung under each wing. It was twice the weight they usually carried and Mark was wondering if their planes could take off with such a heavy load. Their runway was five thousand feet long, and since it was made of pierced plank steel, it was bumpier and produced more drag han the smoother, concrete runway that they were used to. Now, with these loads, their planes would need every foot of it for take-off.

Their take-off technique was to get as close to the back end of the runway as they could, stand on the brakes, run the engine up to full rpm, release the brakes, and accelerate down the runway. A military policeman stood at the far end, wearing a white helmet. His job was to stop traffic from going around the end of the runway while the planes were taking off. Mark knew that when he saw the white helmet go by his canopy, he was out of runway and had to take off. He carefully pulled back on the stick and coaxed the airplane off the ground, just slightly above a stall. There were woods about a half mile from the end of the runway, and he was sweating out whether he would have enough altitude by the time he reached them to clear the trees. Somehow they all survived their take-offs okay, and the bombing mission into Ruhr was a success. However, Lt. Lawrence got shot down during a live-bomb run on a factory. Most of the pilots had only flown about 300 hours so far in their short careers. Lt. Lawrence, on the other hand, had logged 1200 hours, because he had been an instructor for fourteen months in the States. It seemed that survival depended as much on luck as it did on skill. He was a great guy and the squadron was going to miss him.

After their debriefing, the pilots went back to the school house and found the boys waiting for them with their completed laundry. Mark was delighted to receive his bundle clean and neatly folded. He asked the young boy how much it was, and he replied, "Nothing." He said his mother was glad to wash their clothes for them and only needed the soap to do it with. Mark had a lump in his throat, and felt very much moved by such an unselfish gesture.

After living in the school house for a few days, they were moved to a small Belgian country inn that had ten rooms. The military had arranged to rent all of the rooms and use it as a barracks for the pilots. Mark and Bill decided to share one of them.

Mark started receiving letters regularly again from Joanne, and she explained that she had been visiting a sick aunt in St. Louis with her mother for several weeks.

CHAPTER 32

(Belgium)

After putting up their cots and settling down a bit, Bill and Mark went outside to look around and try to get the feel of the place. It was obvious that they were somewhat isolated out in the country, with only a few houses scattered around here and there. Directly next door to the inn, however, was a two-story house with a small store on the first floor. Mark and Bill walked into the store to have a look around, and were surprised to find that practically all the shelves were empty.

They were greeted by a rosy-cheeked girl, probably about eighteen years old, and tried to strike up a conversation with her. She was friendly enough, but didn't speak any English. However, she was soon joined by her older sister who did speak some English. They learned that their names were Anna Marie and Lisa. There obviously was not much to sell in the store because of all the shortages, and the Belgian couple who ran it, along with their daughters, were struggling to keep it going until, hopefully, better times arrived.

It wasn't long before Bill and Mark started visiting the two girls during their time off, and it soon developed into somewhat of a routine. In the evening, they would go over and sit in the kitchen with the girls and their parents. The coal-burning stove was the only source of heat in the two-story house; consequently, everyone sat in the kitchen until retiring to bed. Mark would usually begin to feel sleepy around eight o'clock and excuse himself. Anna Marie, the eighteen-year-old, would walk him to the enclosed porch outside the kitchen, where they would kiss and caress. She would allow him some liberties, but they never went all the way.

Bill always stayed half an hour or so later. He seemed to be getting along very well with Lisa, the older daughter, who was probably around twenty-one, but Bill, would never tell Mark what they did on the porch when they said good night. Somehow, Mark was sure that they had gone further than he and Anna Marie had.

CHAPTER 33

(Belgium)

One morning, Mark had just gotten dressed and was getting ready to go out to the airstrip to fly his afternoon mission. As he waited for his ride in front of the inn, Anna Marie came running out of her house and over to him, very excited. "Come quick," she yelled, waving for him to follow her into their kitchen. She explained that her mother was standing at the sink peeling potatoes when her leg started spurting blood all over the kitchen floor. Apparently the Belgian family believed that an American officer could do anything, and sought him out for help.

When Mark entered the kitchen, the mother was on a stool with something wrapped around her leg. Her husband stood next to her, looking distraught. Lisa was busy wiping up blood from the floor.

Mark thought back to first aid lectures given during training, and remembered the best one was given by an army doctor just before they left for combat.

"If you or your buddy gets wounded, don't worry about all those fancy bandages that they taught you how to make in first aid classes. The most important thing to do is immediately stop the bleeding, and do it any way you can. It would be nice to have a sterile bandage, but there probably won't be one handy. Just use whatever means you have handy to apply pressure: a scarf, a handkerchief, or just put your hand over the wound if there is nothing else available," the doctor had said. "If you don't stop the bleeding, the person will bleed to death. It's as simple as that.

"Next, elevate the wound. Have the injured person sit, or lie down. Make him as comfortable as possible. Remove any

155

foreign objects from the wound if there are any, and then clean it with soap and warm water. Apply some antiseptic on and around it, if at all possible. Once the bleeding is brought under control, wrap the wound to keep out dirt and to maintain pressure. Finally, seek medical aid as soon as possible."

So there Mark was, faced with his first casualty, and it wasn't even in combat.

Mark pulled up a chair so that he could sit in front of the mother; he put her leg up in his lap and looked more closely at what had happened. Evidently, an enlarged varicose vein below the knee had burst.

"My father cut a potato in half and tied it against the wound with the rag," Lisa explained. Mark had never heard of using a potato over a wound before, but as he thought about it, it seemed like a reasonably good idea. A fresh-cut potato would be fairly clean, and certainly a good device for applying pressure.

He asked for another chair and placed her leg so that she could rest her foot on it. This kept the wound elevated. He washed the wound with soap and warm water that Anna Marie provided. He was hoping to apply some antiseptic on and around it to keep it from getting infected. He asked Anna Marie, "Do you have any iodine?"

She didn't understand iodine, but her older sister went over to the kitchen cupboard and came back carrying a small, milky-white glass jar that contained some brownish, dry crystals. Mark thought they might be iodine, but wanted to be sure before applying it to the open wound.

He remembered from freshman chemistry that the test for iodine was the starch test. Iodine turns starch deep blue upon contact. And now, luckily, here before him, was the perfect source of starch—the potato.

He placed a small crystal of the substance on the unused half of the potato, and it immediately began to turn dark blue. Voila! Iodine! But it was dry, and he did not want to place a pure undiluted iodine crystal against the flesh for fear it might burn. What he needed was some alcohol to dilute it with. He looked up at Anna Marie. "Do you have any alcohol?"

Neither girl understood what he meant.

"Whiskey? Cognac? Schnapps?"

When the father heard the word Schnapps, he went back to a cupboard in the next room and produced a bottle which appeared to be a liquor of some sort. Mark took a whiff of it and was satisfied that it definitely had high alcohol content.   He poured a bit into a small saucer, and dissolved some of the iodine crystals. Then painted the wound with the solution, and wrapped it with a clean rag.

He looked at Anna Marie and said, "Your mother should lie down for a few hours, and then to try to see a doctor as soon as possible."

With that, Mark left and caught his jeep ride to the airstrip so as not to miss the briefing for his mission.

Their mission that day was an armed reconnaissance flight deep into hostile territory. Many of their missions were beginning to penetrate deeper and deeper into northern Germany. Although they were having some good results against their ground targets, there was a terrible new threat in the air that grew more ominous every day—the German jet fighter planes. Mark had begun to see their wispy white contrails high in the sky about a month before, and was now seeing them more often. He felt completely helpless and unable to do anything about them. He could neither fly fast enough, nor climb high enough, to catch them.

As the squadron continued on their way to the target area, flying at twenty-five thousand feet and looking for targets, things were relatively quiet. Mark kept scanning the sky, looking for enemy planes. He was suddenly startled by the sight of a German ME-262 jet fighter appearing seemingly out of nowhere, and passing him from behind at his same altitude only a few hundred feet to his right. He was so completely dumbfounded, wondering why the German pilot had not shot him down, that he lost a few precious seconds reacting.

He recovered his senses, and immediately poured on full throttle and swung to the right, so as to slide in behind the jet and started firing. Seeing some of his bullets flashing as they hit the jet's left engine, he thought he was starting to inflict some damage. Then, as if he were tired of being annoyed by this nuisance behind him, the German pilot poured on full power and pulled away from Mark as if he were standing still.

What chances do we have against airplanes like these, Mark thought. If the war doesn't end soon, we'll all be wiped out of the sky.

His attention was snapped back to their mission by a call from ground control. "Browning Squadron, some German army troops are inflicting stiff resistance near the town of Blankenbur and we could use some air support."

Major Adams found the town on his map and led them to it.

"Ground control, we've got the town in sight. Over."

"Roger, Browning. The enemy concentration in the north east sector of the town is putting up stiff resistance. Over."

The squadron started bombing and strafing the target area as they were being directed by the forward controller. Finally they were told that the German troops had surrendered, and were thanked for their help.

Upon returning to the base and completing their debriefing, Bill and Mark hopped in their jeep and headed back to the inn. As they pulled up in front of the building, Anna Marie came running out of her house to meet them, and greeted Mark with a big smile. "We take mother to doctor today. He say everything you do for her is good."

Mark sensed that he was being regarded as some kind of hero by the family, and was a bit embarrassed by it. The father and

Lisa then came out and thanked him. The father then said something in Flemish that Mark didn't understand. Lisa said, "My father want to have you for dinner if you can come Sunday." Mark was hesitant to accept the invitation, because he knew how short of everything they were, especially food. But when the father insisted that he come over for a stewed rabbit dinner, he accepted.

The family had a rabbit hutch behind their house with three rabbits in it. It was the first time that Mark had ever tasted rabbit. It was prepared by the father in a very tasty sauce and was absolutely delicious.

Now the hutch had only two rabbits in it.

CHAPTER 34

(Belgium)

The ability of the Germans to invent and develop new weapons was amazing. In addition to the jet fighters, the Germans came up with three other breakthroughs which could turn the tide of the war if they had enough strength left, and could hold on long enough to use them.

The first was the V-2 rocket, which they were now starting to launch routinely from Germany and send across the English Channel to strike London at will. There was absolutely no defense against this awesome missile. It left a smoke-and-vapor trail as it arched into high altitude at supersonic speeds. Its lack of accuracy and its highly-explosive payload meant that it would land indiscriminately in London and its environs, wreaking havoc on the predominantly civilian population.

Their second invention was the small rocket plane—the ME-163—which could soar to high altitudes extremely fast, but whose fuel was spent in about three minutes. It then essentially became a high speed glider. It did encounter some bombers with effective results. However, it still appeared to be in the experimental stage, and although it did not seem to pose an immediate or significant threat to the Allies, it was a portent of things to come.

The third challenge was the V-1 buzz bomb, essentially a large bomb with crude wings and a simple motor that propelled the craft through a series of controlled explosions. Vanes allowed fuel and air to enter the front of the chamber, there the fuel was lit, and the ensuing explosion forced the forward vanes closed and the combustion products out the rear, thereby propelling the craft for-

ward. It also had a crude guidance system designed to keep it o
a preset course. These, too, were usually aimed at England, but a
other times were aimed at Brussels. They didn't fly at supersoni
speeds like the dreaded V-2 rockets, and some were successfull
shot down by fighter planes as they lumbered across the Englis
Channel. But in order to shoot them down, the fighter had to b
able to see them, and so the Germans usually waited to launc
them until the sky was overcast, and programmed them to fl
within the cloud layer. The engine was so crude and unreliable tha
some of them would quit en route, and land on any villages c
fields which happened to be under their flight path at the time.

The Belgian inn where the pilots stayed seemed to be righ
in the flight path of some of these missiles. Sometimes Mar
would lie in his cot listening to them going over, flying very low—
maybe a few hundred or a thousand feet—just high enough to b
in the overcast. As they passed making their loud putt, putt, pu
sounds, their engines would sometimes stop. Mark always held hi
breath when this happened and prayed for the engine to sta
again. When it did, he felt relieved to hear the putt, putt, pu
again, as the missile proceeded toward its programmed target.

One day, as one of these missiles passed over the inn; th
engine did stop about half a mile away, and didn't start up agair
The consequence was that the bomb blew a large hole in
farmer's field outside a small village, and as far as Mark knew, n
one was hurt.

The Allies were surprised later to learn that the dreade
missile had been designed by a woman.

CHAPTER 35

(Belgium; France)

The war on the ground was progressing favorably for the Allies by this time. The thrust across the north moved forward methodically and ponderously. Meanwhile, in contrast, General Patton, who was more or less supposed to be marking time, further to the south, made a surprising, lightning thrust toward the Rhine River. His Third Army had the constant problem of running short of fuel and supplies, since much of it was being diverted to the north to supply Hodges, and support the British for their planned thrust to the Rhine. In spite of his shortages, Patton's determination seemed to prevail, and he usually surprised everyone with his progress. Upon reaching the river, he was said to have sent the following message to General Eisenhower: "Pissing in the Rhine. Please send gas."

CHAPTER 36

(Belgium; Germany)

Major Adams stood up during the briefing one morning and asked, "Do any of you pilots want to go to the front to be with the army for three days? The army is sending two officers back here to our base, and we were asked to send two officers in exchange, so that each half of the combat forces could see how the other half operates."

Bill and Mark looked at each other. Mark gave him a nod, and Bill gave him a nod in return, then they both raised their hands. The next day, they were on their way to the front lines. They were driven by jeep to an army division headquarters that was located in the basement of a partly-damaged castle near Aachen, Germany.

There they were met by an army captain, Captain Paul Parker. He introduced himself, shook hands with Bill and Mark, and said "I'll be your contact and guide while you're up here at the front with my unit."

He led them into the basement of the castle and said, "We'll have supper here before going forward to join my outfit."

Mark couldn't help but think, I hope this isn't going to be my last supper.

They ate at a long, makeshift table with benches on the sides, and a chair at one end. The commanding general sat at the end, and the rest of the officers filled in on either side. When they had finished eating, Captain Parker took them back up to the courtyard of the castle, where they got into the back seat of a jeep. The driver had been waiting for them, and the captain was going to be sitting next to him. But as the captain was about to get into the jeep, he changed his mind and said, "There are some maps I need to get before we leave. Wait here. I'll be right back." With that, he disappeared back into the castle, leaving the three of them sitting there in the jeep waiting.

They were now close enough to the front lines to hear the booming of an occasional artillery round being fired.

It was getting near dusk, and they listened to the familiar sounds of P-47s which were passing overhead, returning home from their last mission of the day. Bill and Mark were not saying much to each other, but just sitting there wondering what they had gotten themselves into.

As it started getting dark the familiar sounds of the Thunderbolt's engines gradually started being replaced by different sounds—the sounds of unfamiliar aircraft. They were obviously twin-engine airplanes. Mark recognized the sounds, because the engines produced the strange beating noise of two engines which were not quite in synchronization. This was a characteristic sound of German multiengine airplanes.

Bill and Mark looked at each other, and then at the sky. They could just barely make out the outlines of the planes, and were wondering what to do next. They felt rather vulnerable sitting right out there unprotected in the middle of the castle's courtyard.

The airplanes now seemed to be circling high overhead. Suddenly, the sound of the engines from one plane changed, followed by the unmistakable winding up of the propellers that told them the airplane had gone into a dive.

Bill and Mark again shot glances at each other, and Mark barked, "We'd better run for cover!"

As they jumped out of the jeep and started running full speed toward the thick castle wall that surrounded the courtyard, they heard a plane release its bombs and begin its pull-up. They dove for the ground next to the wall, and wiggled as close to it as they could get, and lay there, helplessly. The whistling sound of the bombs grew louder and louder and began to sound as if they were going to land right on top of them.

Then the earth shook beneath them as the bombs hit the ground near a wooden barn in the corner of the courtyard, and the explosions were followed by the sound of shattered lumber being thrown about.

There was a sense of relief to find that they had not been hit, but not for long, because they started to hear the second airplane peel off and enter its dive. This one's engines sounded louder than those of the first plane, and when its bombs were released, the whistling sounded louder. They knew that the last bombs had landed in the courtyard—which was close enough—but these were going to land even closer.

Bill and Mark lay next to each other against the wall, and Mark wished that he could somehow crawl under his steel helmet for protection.

Just then, the second set of bombs hit, and the explosions rocked them, and caused wooden beams, splinters, and dirt to be heaved about, partially covering them with dirt, boards, and stones from the crater.

Bill and Mark were now shaking uncontrollably, and Mark saw Bill's eyes peeking out from under his helmet, looking back at him.

"Boy, its getting cold" he said, shivering.

"Cold, hell," Mark answered. "We're scared!"

They then heard the wooden boards being moved about, and ventured a peek up from under their helmets before the next plane started its dive. They couldn't believe what they saw. There was their driver, climbing among the beams that were strewn about.

"Are those our planes?" he yelled.

"Hell no! They're Germans!" Mark screamed back. "Get down!"

The next plane was already starting its dive, and they could still hear the driver climbing over the boards and rafters. They yelled once more for him to get down, and then pressed as close to each other as possible as they lay on their stomachs, shivering violently.

It came again, the whining engine noise growing louder and louder, and they began to realize that the general's command post in the castle was the target that these Germans were set on knocking out, and that they had practically been sitting on ground zero.

Now some antiaircraft fire could be heard, as the next set of bombs whistled closer and closer.

It was one of the most frightening experiences Mark had ever encountered, to lie there helplessly, listening to your own death approaching, and not being able to do anything about it. This was a ground-war experience. One they didn't get flying. It was much more personal. The noise and the enemy's presence felt more real.

The fourth plane completed its bombing. And somehow, all of the bombs, though landing close by and showering them with debris, had managed to leave them unscathed.

The drone of the German planes began to grow quieter as they returned back to their own base. Gingerly, Bill and Mark pushed their way up through the timber and debris and found that, except for a cut on his cheek, their driver had also survived.

CHAPTER 37

Germany)

It had now grown almost completely dark, and they walked back to their jeep, which was covered with boards and debris. Captain Parker emerged from inside the basement of the castle and asked "Are you guys okay? I'm sorry for the delay. I got held up by a last-minute briefing. It looks like you got some real excitement for your first front line experience.

They uncovered the jeep, used its first aid kit to patch up the driver's cut, and then drove out of the courtyard.

As they started down a narrow country road, they noticed that the telephone line repairmen had already scaled several poles, and were repairing some of the lines that were damaged by the bombs.

"Those are some of the bravest men in the service," the captain said. "They are often up there repairing broken telephone lines during a bombing raid, hanging on a pole, exposed to fire and shrapnel, and totally vulnerable. They realize that one of the most important things in combat to keep soldiers of different units from accidently attacking each other is to have good communications."

They rode along for another half hour on a narrow road that had obviously suffered some bomb damage and showed signs of being hastily repaired. Finally, they pulled into what were the remains of a small village. Only two houses were still standing, and both of those were damaged. GIs were standing around quitly talking, and cleaning and checking their rifles.

"You can tell when the men know they're getting ready to go into a big battle," the captain said, "because normally they'd be kidding and joking around, and yelling at each other."

"We had been pushing the Germans back pretty steadil until they came to the Ruhr River. It is the last major obstac before reaching the Rhine River. The Germans crossed back ove the Ruhr and then turned to put up strong resistance, which ha stopped us in our tracks for several weeks now. Our big push cross the river will start either tonight or tomorrow night."

Mark could understand how the men felt. The worst pa about facing possible death is the waiting. It gives you time to d a lot of thinking, and feel the fear building up. Once in combat, it different, then you're too busy with the mechanics of outsmartin and outfighting the enemy to linger on worrying. Oh, you g scared, very scared. But it's a different kind of fright, a ver intense, exciting, short-term fright, compared to the ponderou gloomy fright that builds up over a long period of time.

The captain led them through a gate into the courtyard a damaged wooden house with a brick foundation. An armed C stood guard at the gate and came to attention as they passed. The went around to the side of the building and down some worn bric steps into what was the cellar of the house.

The cellar was crammed and cluttered, with barely enoug room for three more people. A full colonel sat at a makeshift des looking at some maps laid out before him. Several of his sta were milling around him, and others were busy in other cubicle

Captain Parker briefly introduced them to the colonel, an then Bill and Mark tactfully tried to make themselves as incon spicuous as possible. They could see that all of them were bus with their plans for the big, upcoming offensive.

When they had moved out of earshot, the captai explained to them that the unit's former commanding officer ha been killed three days before by a mortar shell, and that th colonel had arrived only yesterday to be their new CO. Everyon was a bit apprehensive about beginning a big offensive with a ne CO.

At the captain's suggestion, Bill and Mark decided to get some sleep. The captain took them upstairs into what remained of the house. The living room was completely bare of furniture, except for two lonely cots with sleeping bags sitting out in the middle of the floor. The only light in the room was a bit of moonlight coming through the broken window and a hole in the roof. He indicated that they could sleep on the cots and said he would come by for them in the morning.

Bill and Mark were confused as to what they would be doing the next day. They had no infantry experience and were not even carrying rifles. They both wore their .45 pistols hanging from their web belts, along with a canteen of water, and Mark also carried a bayonet. They had both qualified with the .45 on the gunnery range, but knew that it would be no match for a rifle in the field, for distance and accuracy. It would only be effective in a face-to-face encounter with an enemy soldier.

Bill and Mark lost little time climbing into the sleeping bags fully dressed and falling asleep.

CHAPTER 38

(Germany)

The next morning, Captain Parker came back for them. "Let's go get chow," he said as he took them to an outdoor chow line. They got a breakfast of powered eggs, corn beef hash and a good, hot canteen cup full of coffee, which, as usual, burned Mark's lips.

After chow, they climbed back into a jeep with the captain, and drove about half a mile down a small dirt road that was badly damaged by shell fire. The road led them into woods. As they left the jeep and started walking, the captain said that they were now getting quite close to the front line. All the trees in the area had been stripped bare and were damaged by flying shrapnel from the repeated firing of cannons and machine guns during the past few weeks. It gave the landscape an eerie look of desolation. After going a few more steps, they came to a clearing. The captain pointed to it and said, "That's where our commanding officer got killed by a mortar shell three days ago." They continued slowly past the clearing and came to a crude sign nailed to a tree that read: Caution! Front lines, 500 yards.

The captain warned them that they had to be very quiet from that point on, and they proceeded as quietly as they could.

As they continued slowly past the sign, the remains of a badly-damaged house came into view through the haze.

When they approached it, the captain got down into a crouch and signaled for them to do the same. The three of them then came up behind the damaged stone walls of the house, and crept slowly and quietly around the side of it. As they did, the Ruhr River came into view. It became obvious that at one time this had been a nice summer home, built on the banks of the river for a rather well-to-do German family. The captain motioned for them to stop while he peeked around the corner to see if it was clear and then he signaled for them to follow him low and quietly. As they rounded the corner, they saw a fairly well-hidden GI, looking through binoculars at a house in a similar state of disrepair on the other side of the river.

The captain quietly made their presence known to the GI and they scooted behind the pile of rubble beside him. Occasionally, a shot came from the basement window of the house across the river.

"There are two Germans in there," the GI told the captain. "I've had it under observation for several hours, and there might be more, but I can't tell."

The words had no sooner left his lips, than a shot rang out and a bullet ricocheted off the stone wall above their heads. They scooted a bit lower as several more shots hit the wall. The sergeant fired a few shots back at one of the cellar windows, and the shooting stopped. Mark noticed that, in addition to his rifle and binoculars, the sergeant had a field phone. He assumed that the soldier was there primarily to act as a forward observer, and to report front line activity back to the command post from time to time.

Mark looked down at the sizable river and wondered how the troops would get across it in the face of the enemy fire that would be coming at them from the other side. It seemed to him that they would be sitting ducks trying to go across in their inflatable rafts, or while putting up and crossing their bailey bridges. The casualty rate was bound to be very high.

They stayed with the GI another ten minutes, and then carefully made their way back out to the jeep.

When they got back to the center of the bombed-out village, Capt. Parker left them on their own, and went off to take care of some of the things he had to do. After chow, he joined them again. He took them to a field that had the remnants of a wooden building standing on the hillside about a half a mile from the river. There was crude scaffold erected behind its wall, and two army officers stood on the platform, looking through their binoculars. Captain Parker climbed the scaffold to join them, and Mark and Bill followed.

This was obviously an observation post for the field artillery, and the two officers were reporting hits and misses by field phone to the men aiming the big guns from positions further from the river. This helped them make the necessary corrections in their aim. They let Mark look through their binoculars, and he could see a concrete pillbox on the other side of the river, which was part of Hitler's Siegfried Line, a supposedly impenetrable line of fortifications. It was the German counterpart to the French Maginot Line, which when built after World War I, and was supposed to forever prevent the Germans from penetrating into France again. Hitler overcame that formidable defense by simply going around it, first striking through Holland and Belgium, and then turning south into France.

Mark felt that there was a big lesson to be learned here: namely that no country could ever build a defense system so strong, that they could sit comfortably behind it, and depend on it to protect them from a determined enemy.

As Mark watched, artillery shells were pounding a concrete pillbox on the other side of the river, one which held German machine gunners. Some of the shells missed, and some of them hit with a glancing blow and exploded harmlessly in the air. But he was sure that the unrelenting pounding was slowly but surely taking its toll on the concrete structure. The noise and shock inside the small cubical must have been terrifying. The idea, of course, was to knock out the pillboxes so that the American troops could cross the river, climb the hill, and then penetrate deeper inland with less opposition.

The rest of the day, Mark and Bill tried mainly to stay out of everybody's way. When evening finally came, they found themselves trying to go to sleep again in the somewhat eerie, empty house that had the command post in the basement.

CHAPTER 39

(Germany)

If the world ever came to an end by being blown up, it would sound exactly like the thunderous explosions of cannon fire that shattered their sleep in the middle of the night. They bolted upright on their cots, looked at each other, realized that this was the beginning of the big offensive, and wondered what to do. There was one cannon positioned right outside their window, and every time it exploded into action, the walls shook violently, trying their best to collapse. Distant cannons could be heard going off as rapidly as they could be reloaded, aimed, and fired. They were sure the captain would be back to tell them what was going on and what they should be doing, but they were wrong. He was probably somewhere out there with his hands full right now with his own problems, let alone having to worry about them. Should they try to go back to sleep? It was three in the morning. But sleeping was impossible, so they just lay there, shivering and bewildered.

It was still dark when the captain arrived in the morning and took them to chow in the field kitchen. They noticed some men carrying large food containers on a pole between them, and the captain said that they were carrying food to the men in the front lines. Those men were the number one priority, and they were fed warm food whenever it was humanly possible to get it to them.

Mark and Bill were still not sure what their role would be in all this, and the captain implied that it would be best for them to remain there, at the camp, for a while. The next thing they knew, he went off again leaving them to their own devices. Mark walked around the small square a few times, and then decided to walk a ways down the road leading toward the front lines. As he got a few hundred yards out of town, he saw a column of German soldiers walking his way, with their hands clasped on top of their heads. They were being lead by two GIs, one at the head of the column and one at the rear of it. These were obviously some of the first prisoners captured in the offensive, and Mark was curious to see what would become of them. The Germans were marched into the town square, and were ordered to line up into a formation about six men deep.

An American sergeant, who spoke fluent German, stopped in front of each one, asked them certain questions, and instructed each of them to put their possessions into a box he was holding. He was especially looking for knives and other potential weapons.

The Germans were then taken, one at a time, into a room which was all that remained of a bombed-out house. There they remained for about three minutes, and then returned to the formation. Mark decided to go into the room and see what was going on in there.

As he entered, a German soldier was being interrogated by a sergeant at one end of the room, while an American lieutenant sat in front of them and listened. Every once in a while, the lieutenant would ask a question in fluent German.

Mark was fascinated because this was the first time that he had actually seen the enemy up close. The air war was a rather impersonal war in which you never really saw the enemy face-to face. Well, here they were the guys who were trying to shoot his ass off all these months. They looked tired, dejected, and rather docile now.

He had wondered how American officers interrogated prisoners. Somehow, he had visualized an officer pacing back and forth in front of the prisoner, screaming questions and threats, with a sergeant occasionally beating the prisoner with a bludgeon. But there was none of that. No screaming, no threats, just a few questions being asked of each man, perhaps lingering a little longer once in a while on a man who seemed to offer some information which was more valuable than what the others had.

Mark moved inconspicuously to the back of the room, and seated himself on a pile of rubble. In a few minutes, another person wandered in and sat on a box near him. As they sat there listening, Mark occasionally glanced at the man next to him, trying to determine his rank, but he couldn't see any insignia on his jacket.

As he continued to observe the interrogation, the visitor, who apparently understood the German being spoken, said almost as if he were reflecting out loud, "It's the same story here as it was in Italy. None of them claim to have ever shot at an American!"

Mark couldn't think of anything to say, but took the opportunity to take a better look at him, and then realized that he was a war correspondent.

Mark finally left the room and went out to look for the chow line and for Bill. He found both at the same place. Capt. Parker also appeared, and said that it was time for him to rejoin his unit in battle and for them to head back to their squadron. Mark asked him if he knew who the war correspondent was that he had run into. He said, "Yes, that was Bill Mauldin, who draws the popular cartoon, 'The Sad Sack' for the Stars and Stripes newspaper."

They thanked Capt. Parker for his help, bade him farewell, and then got in their jeep and were driven back to Belgium.

CHAPTER 40

Belgium)

One surprising benefit of being stationed where they were n Belgium was being able to get a good hot bath at the main building at the entrance to the coal mine. There, the mining company permitted the enlisted men to use the showers on the first loor, where the miners showered, and the officers to use the bathubs upstairs, where the foreman and managers bathed. There vere about a dozen tubs which were continuously being used, and vere kept clean after each bath by a cleaning lady. The service vas being provided for them by the mining company as a token of ppreciation for helping to liberate their country, and there wasn't ny charge for the bath. There was usually a short wait when they got there, but they didn't mind because it gave them an opportunity to talk to pilots from the other nearby squadrons and compare notes on how they were doing. It was during one of these waits hat Mark ran into Willie Thompson, and asked him how he was oming along. Mark hadn't seen him since he had gotten burned y trying to start a fire in his stove using gasoline.

"Not so hot," Willie replied.

"Oh, what seems to be the problem?" Mark asked a bit ewildered. He looked okay, except for a scar on his cheek which Mark didn't remember seeing before.

"Well it's like this," he went on to say. "Our commanding fficer asked us if anyone wanted to go to the front for a few days, nd I volunteered. Well, I ended up in the front lines during a batte, and was lying down aiming my rifle at a German, when I sudenly got hit. The bullet actually just grazed me, hitting my thumb vhere it rested on the gun stock, and my cheek which was pressed gainst the stock right behind it."

"Wow! Were you laid up because of it?"

"Yeah, I was grounded for almost a month, until my thumb and cheek healed, but I'm okay now."

Mark asked him how many missions he had flown, and he said a total of twelve. Mark had flown forty-two by this time, and wondered if poor Willie would ever finish the required number of missions so that he could go home.

A week later, the squadron got orders to move again. As the front lines moved forward, the fighter bases always moved up behind them.

This time, they were being sent into Germany near the town of Kitzingen.

Mark and Bill said good-bye to their Belgian friends and family, with whom they had become very close. As they got into their planes and left, Bill and Mark flew over Anna Marie and Lisa's house, and both did a slow roll over their rooftop, saying good-bye in their own way.

CHAPTER 41

(Germany)

The airbase at Kitzingen sat in a valley that had a castle perched on a plateau overlooking it. Their new base had been an active German airbase only a few weeks before being captured. It was taken well intact, so the squadron had comfortable barracks to sleep in.

They were now starting to fly missions into southern Germany and Austria.

On Mark's second mission, his engine started acting up, and he had to abort and return to his base alone. This, however, turned out to be a more serious problem than he expected. An overcast had moved into the area, and he had to make an instrument let-down through the cloud layer—something he always felt uncomfortable doing. In addition, there was the problem of trying to figuring out where he was, since he couldn't see the ground, and there were no radio aids in the combat area to help him.

He entered the top of the clouds at twelve thousand feet, and glued his eyes to the instrument panel. He made a single, needle width turn until he was heading west, and then started a thousand feet per minute letdown, hoping to break out in the clear before reaching five thousand feet. But the cloud layer was thicker than he expected, and he still could not see the ground. He had no idea how high the hills were in that area, but he reluctantly continued his let down—three thousand feet, two thousand, one thousand—and still no breakthrough. He knew that there were some hills higher than that in the area but had no choice but to cautiously let down a bit further. He began to see a slight thinning of the clouds and carefully let down another hundred feet. By some miracle, he found himself flying right over the Danube River, with the hills on either side disappearing up into the overcast. Had he come down a few thousand feet to either side of the river, he would have flown into the hills. Someone up there was looking out for me, he thought, but wondered just how long that same kind of luck, which had carried him through forty-five combat missions, could possibly continue.

Mark flew along the river, skimming under the clouds and looking for signs of some landmark that would help tell him where he was. Navigating while flying a fighter at that low an altitude was very difficult. The scenery went by so fast that there was practically no time to find what he saw on the map, and by the time he did find it, he would be way past it. The flying itself also took a lot of attention in order to anticipate what was ahead and keep from flying into it.

Mark finally spotted a bridge up ahead which he thought might be the one at Regensburg. He took a quick glance at his map, and felt rather sure that it was. He knew there was a field on the southern edge of town, and decided to make a go for it. As he passed over the bridge, he banked hard left, skirted a hill and got a glimpse of the field peeking out from under the overcast ahead. He landed successfully and spent the night on the base. In the morning, the weather had cleared and he was able to refuel and fly back to his base at Kitzingen.

CHAPTER 42

(Germany: May 7, 1945)

The squadron had only been at Kitzengen ten days when they got the news they had all been praying for.

Germany surrenders! The war in Europe was over!

The announcement over the loudspeaker told everyone in the squadron to meet in front of the commanding officer's quarters at 10 a.m. for a special announcement.

They were all gathered there as Major Adams came out onto his balcony and said that he had a message to read from General Dwight D. Eisenhower, Supreme Allied Commander, Europe. The message started by saying that on this day, the German High Command signed an unconditional surrender which immediately brought an end to the war in Europe.

The cheer was deafening. Each man turned to shake hands with the man next to him, and immediately felt that a great burden had been lifted from his shoulders.

The commanding officer also had a big smile and waited patiently until the roar died down. He then went on to read: "The general wished that he could thank each of you personally for the part that you played in bringing about this great victory.

"He wants to emphasize, however, that in our victory, we are Americans, and in keeping with the high standards of American morality, he expects everyone to behave in an honorable manner. There will be no looting or any other unacceptable behavior tolerated from the conquering troops. Nor will there be any fraternization with the German people." This statement took them

somewhat by surprise, and Major Adams felt that he should clar
ify it slightly. "That means, among other things, that you do nc
date German girls." He finished his talk by saying that they woul
celebrate the occasion with a parade at one o'clock the followin
afternoon, and that everyone would participate.

The pilots all celebrated that night at the officers' clut
drinking and shooting craps until the wee hours of the morning
and Mark, for the first time since being in Europe, ended up
winner.

CHAPTER 43

(Germany May 7, 1945)

The war in Europe was over, yet there was still a fierce war going on in the Pacific against Japan. Mark and the rest of the pilots realized that it would only be a matter of time before they would be sent into combat there. They also realized that it would be intense fighting because the Japanese were dedicated to fight to the bitter end without surrendering. For the time being, however, they would savor the end of the war on the European front.

* * * *

What is it like on the day a war ends?

Well, the first thing to worry about is that someone out there may not have gotten the news yet.

It was a strange feeling to walk down to the flight line and see everyone relaxed. The enlisted men had a baseball game going, and the men in the antiaircraft emplacement were sitting on the edge of the revetment with their shirts off, sunning themselves as they watched the game.

As Mark stood there, drinking in the wonderfully changed mood of the place, a curious sight appeared over the horizon, causing every man to freeze in his tracks.

There, coming in at treetop level, was something almost unbelievable—a red, bi-wing, World War I vintage, open-cockpit German airplane. It headed over the field, rocking its wings back and forth, indicating that it wanted to land.

The troops stopped their game and stood gawking as the plane circled the field. The men in the antiaircraft emplacement leaned against their gun, bewildered as to what to do. Yesterday they would not have hesitated to shoot it down. But now, the war was over. Or was it?

The plane touched down and taxied toward the hangar, and then cut its engine. The operations officer and two enlisted men with rifles went out to the picturesque aircraft, and waited for the pilot to dismount. He was an older man, gray-haired, rather distinguished-looking, and dressed in civilian clothes. He was escorted into the operations office by the two men, and questioned by the operations officer.

It turned out that he lived on a farm about fifty miles to the east of the base, and feared that it would come under Russian control, so he decided to flee the area, and fly over to surrender to the Americans, who he felt would treat him in a much more humane fashion. He had restored and maintained the old World War Fokker C.VII as a hobby, and had kept it in working order in his barn for years. When the war ended, he flew it west, and there he was, with his museum piece in mint condition.

The ball game resumed, but 15 minutes later a Messerschmitt Me-109 appeared. This was the deadly German fighter that most of the pilots had tangled with at one time or another. The plane made a somewhat bumpy landing and came to a stop. A young German lieutenant jumped out of the cockpit and immediately ran to the side of its fuselage. He lost no time in undoing a few fasteners and opening a hinged door near the tail. Much to everyone's surprise, he reached in and pulled his wife out of the small cramped space. It turned out that he, too, had decided to escape from the oncoming Russians, and bring his wife with him as he surrendered to the Americans. She had to straddle the control wires as she squatted in the tortuous position, and nearly froze when he climbed to high altitude.

Just when things were beginning to calm down and the men were starting to play ball again, a Focke-Wulf 190 appeared. This was the kind of dreaded fighter that Mark had made a head on pass with once near the Rhine river.

The pilot was a German colonel, and showed none of the meekness of a conquered soldier. On the contrary, he arrogantly tossed his Luger pistol to one of the MPs, introduced himself to the operations officer with a click of his heels, and wanted to challenge the commanding officer to an air duel, he in his Focke-Wulf and the CO in his Thunderbolt. Needless to say, he was taken into custody.

So the war was over and there were no more missions to worry about. But something was wrong. The pilots were being summoned to the briefing room. Why? They expected to have several days to unwind before having to fly again, and then there would only be training missions.

The drone of the conversation in the room came to a halt when someone barked, "Attention!" as the CO entered. There was a period of silence as he looked around the room, then he spoke.

"Gentlemen, we have one more mission to fly."

They all turned to look at each other in bewilderment. The war in Europe was over. How could they have one more mission to fly?

The CO slapped his pointer against the large map on the wall behind him. "We are here at Kitzingen, Germany." He then slid the pointer down toward the southeast almost to the point where the map ended. "There is a prisoner of war camp located here at Ebensee, Austria. It is located so far behind the front lines that our ground troops haven't been able to get there yet. Headquarters has directed us to fly our squadron over the camp at rooftop level so that the prisoners will get a moral boost by seeing American planes, and realize that we know where they are and that we are coming to get them." The mission seemed easy enough. At least no one would be shooting at them.

"There are two slight problems," the CO went on to say. "One is the distance. It is just about the limit of our range. Fuel will be a concern, especially in view of the tricky maneuvering we'll have to do around the Alps. The second problem is the awkward location of the camp itself. It's on the edge of a lake, Lake Traunsee which is located at the foot of the mountains, the Alps. We could go in on the deck, fly over the lake, and buzz the camp. The only trouble with that is we would be immediately facing two tall mountains, which would guarantee disaster. The other way is to enter the Alps from the west, skirt our way around the valleys and between the peaks until we come to the narrow pass that opens up on to the lake. Since the village will immediately appear below us, we will have to make a steep dive to get down to it. We'll then pass over the camp, getting as low as we can without hitting anything, and continue across the lake and head for home. Take-off will be at 800 hours tomorrow morning. Your assignments are posted."

Mark was assigned to be the element leader in the second flight. It will seem strange to be flying deep into Germany and Austria without anyone shooting at us, he thought.

May 8, 1945 is proclaimed V-E Day

They took off at 8:00 o'clock sharp the next morning and flew for two and a half hours into Austria. As the Alps rose in the distance, Mark was glad that the job of navigating fell on the squadron leader, because the mountains all looked alike to him, and a wrong turn up a dead end valley could be fatal to the whole squadron.

They entered the mountains between two peaks and started snaking their way through the valleys. As it narrowed and the mountains grew taller, Mark kept glancing out of the corner of his eyes, feeling his wing tips almost scraping some of the sheer cliffs. He felt the whole formation tightening up. When he dared to glimpse up he was awed by the breathtaking scenery. He was now breaking out in a sweat from the tension of flying a tight formation in such close quarters. The squadron started a gentle turn to the left skirting around a precipice, and then steepened their turn considerably. Suddenly there appeared before them a most breathtaking sight. Revealing itself within the narrow gap was a beautiful, long lake which mirrored the surrounding peaks. At the nearest edge of the lake lay the camp, their destination.

They immediately went into a steep dive to lose 2,000 feet as quickly as possible. As they passed over the camp at rooftop level, he noticed a whiff of smoke coming from one of the chimneys. As they continued out over the lake, Mark also noticed that there was still ice around its perimeter.

Then the unbelievable happened! The plane in front of him hit the water, pulled up briefly, veered to the right, entered the water again, and sunk like a rock. Mark glanced over his shoulder as he passed the point of impact, and noticed a head bobbing in the water.

He's safe! was Mark's first reaction, but then he started to think about how far he was from shore. The Thunderbolt's wing span was forty-one feet, and he was about four or five wing lengths from shore. To make matters worse, the shore was rimmed with ice. Another problem was that in Europe, pilots seldom wore Mae West's or carried a dinghy, because they never flew over any large body of water. Whoever it was could be in serious trouble.

When they returned to their base, everyone gathered in the briefing room to find out who the downed pilot was. It was Henry Mohr. He was one of the two married fighter pilots in the squadron, and was well-liked by everyone. Whenever they asked Henry what married life was like, he would say how great it was, how his wife always had his shoes shined, and his uniform clean and pressed and laid out for him in the morning. They always wondered if it was really true, and fantasized that someday their wives would be like Henry Mohr's wife.

Did he survive? They talked about the chances, but there were too many variables, and they figured they would just have to wait to find out.

About 9 p.m., that night, the squadron got a call from a forward army medical unit. They said that Henry Mohr had been fished out of the lake by two women who happened to be on the shore near a row boat, and close to where Henry went in. They rowed out, pulled him out of the icy water, and took him to a field hospital. Henry was resting and would be back in a few days.

When he returned, they all gathered around to hear his story.

"After skimming over the rooftops of the prisoner of war camp, I got just a bit too low over the lake and my prop hit the water. While I still had enough speed, I was able to get airborne again briefly. But my propeller blades were bent and the plane vibrated violently. In the short time I had before reentering the water, I tried to maneuver the plane closer to the shore. Just before I hit again I got the canopy open. Immediately the heavy engine sank, pulling the nose of the plane straight down. I undid my safety belt and pushed myself out of the cockpit as it filled with water. My biggest worry was being sliced in half by the tail when it whizzed past my head as the plane sank. At first the parachute helped to keep me afloat, but when it got soaked, it got heavy, and I worked my way out of it. As I fought to keep my head above water, I realized that I had to get my GI shoes off before I could swim ashore. I started struggling with the laces, but they were double-knotted and hard to untie. I was beginning to get tired and just keeping my head above water was wearing me out. I finally got one shoe off but ended up so exhausted that I decided to give up and let myself drown. When I got my mouth and nose full of water and couldn't breathe I decided, No! I've got to fight to live. I fought again; gasping for air, but in a short time my arms ached and my energy was gone. I again decided to give up. Then the survival instinct took over again and I decided to fight. Finally passed out. If it wasn't for those two women, I would be dead. I've often heard that if a man goes down three times he drowns, and never knew what it meant. Now I know. However, I was told that I went down at least six times. I guess I've just got more determination than most or maybe I've got more to live for."

CHAPTER 44

Germany)

   With time on their hands, now that they had no missions to
ly, the pilots started exploring some of the buildings near the
ase. One appeared to have been a small factory. A room in its
asement was filled about three feet deep with brass coins. Mark
nd Bill gathered up a handful each, and noticed that they were
rinkled. When they took some of them back to the base, they
earned from their intelligence officer that the building had been
used to manufacture brass parts for submarines. The Germans had
aken the brass money from countries they had occupied, and ran
hem through a crinkling machine so that no one could spend the
noney before they got around to melting it down for brass bear-
ngs.

   Rumor had reached the base that there was a large ware-
ouse in Munich that was loaded with German uniforms, insignia,
guns, and equipment, and if anyone wanted some souvenirs, they
vere there for the taking.
   Bill and Mark got permission to take a jeep and a two-
vheel trailer down to Munich, which was about 175 miles away to
he southeast. They would try to bring back some souvenirs for the
quadron. When they got to the warehouse area, they found that
he huge facility consisted of a complex of large buildings which
ad been the main supply center for the German army, navy, and
ir force. In one building, they found uniforms and insignia. They
ried on different uniforms, epaulets, and decorations, making
hemselves colonels and generals. They tried on different hats and
elmets and pinned wings onto their uniforms and medals on to

their chests, and finally scooped helmets full of insignia into the trailer and threw in some uniforms, hats, and helmets.

Between the buildings were huge stacks of rifles. When the war ended, German soldiers were required to march by in single file and toss their rifles onto these piles. They loaded six of the rifles into the trailer, which was all they had room for. In another building, they found cannon parts, including a barrel for the large gun of a battleship.

When they got back to camp, everyone helped themselves to what they wanted, and if they didn't get enough, they could always go back to Munich and get more.

CHAPTER 45

(Germany)

Within a few days, Mark and the others found themselves transferred to another base on the edge of the southern town of Straubing, located on the Danube River.

There they found the remains of a prison camp, located next to the base where the Germans had kept captured Russians who worked in various factories in the area. The prisoners were, of course, released when the war ended, and most of them had left for their homes on foot. It was now a common sight on all of the main roads to see a continuous line of displaced people walking back to their homelands—wherever that may be. The lines stretched as far as the eye could see in either direction.

For some reason, the Russian women had not yet left the base, and were moved from the squalor of the prison camp into one of the empty troop dormitories. Perhaps the army was waiting for some trucks to become available to transport the women, so that they would not have to make the long walk to their homes.

At any rate, the women were moved into the building right next to the one which housed the pilots, and they soon found themselves waving to each other from the windows.

As it grew dark, several of the pilots decided to go over to the ladies' barracks and see if they could work up a bit of action of some kind. When they reached the door, however, they were greeted by a rather husky, matronly lady who seemed to have assumed the position of being in charge of the group. She was surrounded by about a dozen or so girls, who watched and giggled as they tried to make themselves understood. It was soon obvious that they could speak no English (and the Americans, of course, spoke no Russian), and that the matron was not going to let any of her charges out, nor was she going to let any of the pilots in. They returned disillusioned, back to their own barracks. The next day the women were being moved to new quarters somewhere in the town of Straubing.

Mark had all but forgotten about the incident when two days later, he was alone in his room and happened to look out of the window. There was one of the Russian girls, standing on the ground right outside of his window, looking up at him. Mark signaled for her to come closer, and when she did, he reached down for her. She reached up to grasp his hands, and he pulled her up through the open window.

He couldn't get over it. There he was, alone in his room with a rather pretty, rosy-cheeked Russian girl, who appeared to be about sixteen years old. He didn't know what to say, and nor did she, and they wouldn't have understood each other anyway. Mark normally had some chocolate bars, and a can of Vienna sausages or sardines around, but not that day, and he couldn't think of anything he had to offer her.

They looked at each other and he pulled her to him. She did not resist. He bent over and kissed her. She did not object, but she was rather passive about it. He caressed her very large breasts and she stood there passively, accepting his advances.

How strange, he thought. How awkward. What if one of the other pilots walks in on us?

They always left the doors open to the hallway, but he decided that he had better go close his door while she was there.

He went back to the girl and unbuttoned her dress, and led her over to his bed. They had both gotten undressed and just started to lie down when he heard someone opening his door. He jumped out of bed, grabbed some clothes, held them in front of himself, and ran to the door just as Lt. Bayer started to walk in. Mark startled him as he rushed to stop him. Bayer stopped in his tracks, and looked at Mark, a bit bewildered.

"Bob, I've got a woman in here," he said. "How about getting lost for a bit?"

He looked at Mark for a moment in disbelief, and then it sunk in.

"Oh. Okay." And he turned around and left.

Mark and the Russian girl made love in action only. She was completely and unemotionally submissive, and when they were through, she got dressed. He apologized for not having any candy or anything to give to her, but that didn't seem to matter to her in the least. He lowered her back out through the window, the way she came in, and that was the last he ever saw of her. He often thought about her walking all the way out to the base, a distance of three miles or so, and then walking all the way back, just for the few moments they had spent together, and felt sorry that he wasn't able to give her something of material or emotional value in return.

CHAPTER 46

Germany)

Although their barracks and mess hall were at Straubing, he pilots did their flying off a grass airfield at Passau, a small own a few miles away on the Austrian border. It was the first time hat they had ever flown a P-47 off a grass field, and in spite of heir apprehension, the take-offs seemed to work surprisingly well or such a heavy airplane. The field had been used by the Germans for many years, and had survived unscathed because, from he air, it looked just like any other grass field in the countryside, nd had gone unnoticed by the Allies.

There were about a dozen small gliders parked around the dge of the field that immediately intrigued the pilots. They were ather flimsy, high-winged crafts, and the pilot sat perched, out in he open, on a seat mounted above the landing skid. They learned hat these were the gliders in which the German Luftwaffe pilots irst learned to fly since, after World War I, the Geneva Convenion had forbidden them from making powered aircraft. When Adolph Hitler finally became powerful enough to ignore the lecree, he had powered planes built by the thousands. By then, no ne had the nerve to stop him.

The American pilots had a ball with these small gliders. They got them airborne by being towed behind a jeep, and when hey reached three or four hundred feet of altitude, they disconected the cable and glided a few hundred yards until the glider inally landed on its skid.

It took less than a week to wreck all of them. The most ommon accident was getting airborne, trying to make a turn, and hen spinning in. Luckily, no one was seriously hurt, even though

199

the pilot sat precariously vulnerable out on the nose of the flims
craft.

Around the corner, hidden by a grove of trees, there was
large German bomber—one of the few that Hitler had built wit
the intention of bombing New York City.

Mark couldn't help but think of how that would hav
changed the American perspective on the war, since throughou
two world wars, there had never been a bomb or an enemy shell h
an American city.

CHAPTER 47

(Austria)

Mark had now completely stopped getting letters from Joanne and, as hard as he tried, he still couldn't get her out of his mind and it worried him deeply.

Their flying was now limited to an occasional training flight, and time hung heavy on the young, healthy, energetic American pilots. So one day Mark and Dan Borrowski decided to go hitchhiking and explore some of Austria. Hitchhiking was not a problem, because the first GI truck that came down the road would always stop and give them a lift. When they got hungry, they needed only to look for a GI unit where a bunch of soldiers were gathered. It was no trouble finding a chow line around noon or supper time, and they were always welcome and fed without any problem.

They reached the town of Linz, Austria and checked into a small hotel, which was one of the very few remaining buildings. Somehow it seemed to have survived the war surprisingly well. Most of the rest of the town was in shambles.

They started walking around to look the place over, but there was very little of interest to see. As they came to an intersection of two main streets, they stopped for traffic. It was being directed by an MP standing on a box at the center of the intersection. When he signaled for them to cross, he also motioned for them to approach him. He seemed to want to tell them something.

When they reached him, he slurred, "Hey, Lieutenant, you want some torpedo juice?"

Dan and Mark looked at each other, and then at the MP, who was obviously a bit drunk. Dan shrugged his shoulders and asked, "What's torpedo juice?"

The MP went on to explain that when the American troops entered Linz, they found many of the railroad cars in the yard loaded with alcohol destined for use in propelling German rockets. The doctors tested it and found it fit for human consumption. The MP went on, "It's really good stuff, there's plenty of it, and if you want a gallon or two, you can get some from my buddies at the MP barracks."

Mark and Dan looked at each other and shrugged. "Well, we don't want a whole gallon, but it would be nice to get a bottle. Oh, by the way, do you know where I can get a Luger?" Mark asked.

"Yeah, you can probably buy one off an MP down there. I've seen several of 'em floating around."

Mark had always wanted a Luger, which was the German officers' pistol. It was more accurate and had a nicer balance to it than the American .45. Mark had been hoping to get one before he left for the Pacific.

With the aid of the MP's directions, they made their way down to the MP barracks a few blocks away. They soon found themselves in a room with several MPs that were also feeling no pain, and seemed happy to share a bottle of torpedo juice with them. Someone also came up with a Luger for Mark, for which he paid twenty-five dollars. They thanked the MPs, and took their bottle and pistol and headed back to the main street.

As Dan and Mark were walking down the street, they caught sight of a very beautiful blond, blue-eyed young girl, about seventeen years old, walking toward them. As they started to pass her, Dan stopped her and started talking to her in broken German. Mark immediately became uncomfortable and reminded Dan about the no fraternization decree, which made any association with the Germans and Austrians forbidden. Dan shrugged it off and continued talking to her as Mark looked up and down the street nervously. In no time, Dan had her engrossed in a conversation and seemed oblivious to his admonishment.

"I'm going on back to the hotel," Mark finally said. "See you later."

"Okay."

Once back at the hotel, there was nothing to do. It had been a long day anyway, so he went to sleep on one side of the big bed, and left plenty of room on the other side for Dan whenever he came in.

He must have just fallen asleep when he heard the door opening.

In walked Dan with the beautiful Austrian girl. Mark turned briefly and said hello, then turned back on his side facing away from them, so as not to impose on their privacy.

Dan, I don't know how you do it, he thought to himself, but it looks like you did it and got away with it.

As he lay there trying to go to sleep, he couldn't help hearing some mumbling as they kissed and caressed, and then sensed them undressing. He soon felt the bed moving as they crawled in beside him. With his back toward them, he could visualize their every move. Twisting, squirming, kissing, caressing and fondling. Finally, there was the rocking of the bed in a steady rhythm, and then a final, muffled moaning as Dan reached his climax. Then silence.

All three of them lay there quietly for some time. When it seemed that they had fallen asleep, Mark slowly turned to face them. The girl was lying between the two of them, and he could feel the warmth of her body permeating the space between them under the sheets.

Mark normally had a creed that he never fooled with another guy's girl; but it seemed that Dan had gone to sleep, and he somehow sensed that she had not. He reached over and slid his arm around her waist, and she continued to lie there motionless. He moved his hand up to her breasts and rubbed his fingers over her nipples. She stirred a bit, but remained very still. Then he pulled her toward him, and she came willingly.

They were now facing each other, with their nude bodies pressed against each other, as he stroked her back and squeezed her.

When he kissed her, she responded warmly. He felt like a heel for doing this to Dan's girl, but there was no stopping them now. They made love several times, and then fell asleep in each other's arms.

In the morning they gave her some Hershey bars, and then she was gone. Dan seemed somewhat disturbed, not by the fact that Mark had seduced his girl, but because he had kept her on his side of the bed all night.

"All you had to do was reach for her," Mark said.

Dan seemed to get over it right away, and they were soon headed back to their base together.

CHAPTER 48

Germany)

Everyone was enjoying their newfound freedom, now that he pressures of combat were over. They were still scheduled to fly a few practice flights several times a week, so the first thing they did in the morning was to look at the flight schedule board to see f they were slated for that day. If not, they lolled around the barracks, or took off to see some of the countryside. Of course, they all realized that it was a false sense of placidity, for in another part of the world, there was still a hot and heavy war going on against he Japanese, and it was only a matter of time before they would be in it.

All kinds of rumors were floating around as to who would be sent to the Pacific, and how they would be sent there. First they were told that they might go together as a squadron, by troop ship. The latest rumor had it that the older pilots with over thirty-five missions would be going back to the States for a thirty-day leave before being sent to fight the Japanese. So now they also checked he bulletin board every day for orders that might enlighten them n some way.

A group of names appeared one morning, listing those who would be sent to Paris for processing prior to boarding a troop ship, but it didn't say whether the troop ship would be going to the Pacific or to the States. Mark's name was among them.

CHAPTER 49

(Germany; France)

Within three days, Mark found himself in the back of another GI truck bound for Munich. This time, he couldn't help but reflect on how different this ride was compared to the one that had taken him into combat just under a year ago. Then, he and thirteen others were riding the other way, freezing, scared, and bewildered, as they were being delivered to their squadrons. Out of the fourteen, only six had survived, and Mark was amazed and thankful to be one of them.

When they reached Munich, they were loaded onto a C-47 transport and flown to Paris. Much to his surprise, they were housed for processing back at the Chateau de Rothschild, very much the same way that they had been processed before going into combat.

One thing they had to do at the chateau was to get their baggage checked to make sure that they weren't taking any unauthorized materials to the States with them. Mark wasn't sure what sort of items they were looking for, and was bothered by the thought that they might not let him take his German Luger, and the two other pistols he had acquired, home with him. Well, it turned out that the procedure for getting their baggage checked consisted of bringing their B-4 bag and their foot locker up to the main building when their name was called over the PA system. There they placed them open on a table so that an inspector could look through them. It didn't take a genius to figure out that if there was something you didn't want the inspector to see, you simply left it back in your room, and then put it back in your baggage when you returned. Almost everyone did this with their pistols. Mark never heard of anything ever being denied or confiscated.

Mark found that he was also allowed to ship his German rifle back to the States, and even got help making a wooden crate for it in the workshop located in the compound.

The pilots were restricted to the chateau area, probably so that the administrators could keep them together as a group, and would not have to go looking for them individually when they were summoned to be sent to their troop ship.

There was a wall around the grounds of the chateau, but there were no guards posted. So Mark and Bill decided to scale the wall, with the help of a nearby tree, one afternoon. It had a sizable limb that overhung the wall and afforded some cover to keep them from being seen from the chateau as they made their escape. When they dropped to the sidewalk on the other side, they walked a few blocks and caught a street car which was heading for the center of Paris.

They eventually had to transfer to another one. As they boarded it, they found it crowded. However, just inside the door was a very attractive French girl. Mark didn't know what prompted him to say it out loud; maybe it was because he thought no one would understand him. Anyway, he blurted out to Bill "Wow! A real princess!"

The girl must have understood him, because her eyes caught his, and he detected a slight smile. He took this as a brief flirtation.

He and Bill made their way toward the back of the street car, but the girl stayed up front near the door. Their eyes met several times, and Mark made up his mind that it was more than just a flirtation. He was getting a downright invitation.

He turned to Bill and said, "I'm getting off when she does. I'll see you back at the chateau."

He gradually worked his way forward, and when the street car reached the stop where she got off, he got off. They paused to et the street car move on, and then he turned to her and asked, "Do you speak English?"

"A leetle bit."

"Where are you going?"

"Back to my room. I jest feenish shopping."

As he walked along with her, she appeared to be very friendly, and said that her name was Nanette. When they reached the door of her apartment building, he waited while she opened it. She stood in the open door for a moment, then turned back to him, and gave a slight nod to indicate that it was okay for him to come in.

They went upstairs to the second level, where she unlocked the door to her room. It was not a large room, but it was neat and clean, and the sunshine was pouring in through the sheer curtains, which were billowing in a balmy breeze.

She took off her jacket, and he came up behind her and slid his hands around her waist, and kissed her on the ear and neck. She turned to him and met him in a warm kiss.

How lovely and radiant she was. He tightened his arms around her, pressing her tightly against him as they kissed again. They soon found themselves on the bed. They paused long enough to get undressed and slid under the covers.

Then she did something that he had never seen before. She was leaning against a pillow, and the covers were down to her waist, exposing her beautiful bosom. She looked at him out of the corner of her eye with an impish stare and said, "Look."

He watched as she caressed one of her breasts, and gently but firmly squeezed it. Lo and behold—milk came out of her nipple! Mark was astonished, but lost no time in putting her nipple into his mouth and sucking some milk from her. It was a rare and delightful experience.

She went on to tell him that she had just had a baby by a French lieutenant, and that it had been placed in an orphanage.

They spent several hours together, and after a while she grew very quiet, as if in deep thought. She suddenly came up with a proposal that startled him.

"You get out of army and stay with me."

He laughed, "I can't do that. How would I make a living?"

"You don't have to worry about that. I will take care of you."

He thought about it for a minute, and said, "How can you take care of me?" Then it finally dawned on him. She was a prostitute.

"Oh," he said, "you'll do it by sleeping with other men."

"Well, it is the only way I know how," she responded.

They lingered together a while longer, and then she told him that if he wanted to see her again, he could find her by going to the Casino de Paris after five o'clock.

They then got dressed and left in separate directions.

Mark caught the streetcar back to the Chateau de Rothschild and climbed the wall to get back in. Bill had already returned earlier.

CHAPTER 50

(France)

The powers in Washington finally reached a decision and announced the long awaited reassignment policy. If a pilot had accumulated a certain number of points, based on the number of missions he had flown plus some other factors, he would be sent back to the States for thirty days' leave, and then be sent to fight in the Pacific. If he had less than that, he would be sent directly to the Pacific.

Mark had more than enough points, so he would be going home for thirty days.

The lines for the telephones were always long, but after an hour and a half's wait, Mark was able to put through a call to Jackson, Mississippi. Then a familiar voice on the other end said, "Hello."

It was Mrs. Williams, Joanne's mother.

"Hello, Mrs. Williams. It's Mark Andrews. How are you?"

"I'm fine, Mark. It's nice to hear your voice. How are you?"

"I'm great. I just got some wonderful news today. I'm coming home by troop ship for thirty days' leave before going to the Pacific. May I speak to Joanne?"

"She's not here, Mark."

"I guess that the fact that I have suddenly stopped getting letters from her means that she has found someone else."

"Well, I think that she should tell you the situation rather than me. Why don't you call her when you get here?"

Their conversation was then interrupted by the operator, "Your three minutes are up, sir. Please signal when through."

"Okay, Mrs. Williams, I've got to go, good-bye."
"Good-bye, Mark."

CHAPTER 51

Belgium)

In a few days, Mark was sent to a temporary base which had been erected on the beaches of Antwerp, Belgium. It was alled Camp Lucky Strike. There, he and several thousand other oldiers were billeted in tents, and waited for their turn to board a roop ship bound for the States. The weather was warm and pleasnt, but there wasn't much for them to do there. They cleaned their niforms in gasoline, and checked the bulletin board every day for mbarkation orders. If they were not listed by three in the afteroon, they were free to catch a bus into town and explore ntwerp.

For some reason, Bill had not been sent to the port of mbarkation at the same time as Mark, and it was the first time hat they had been separated since he joined his squadron. He issed Bill, but soon made the acquaintance of a pleasant fellow amed Capt. Walter Benet, and they ended up going into Antwerp ogether. They walked around the city, took some pictures, and ried to learn something about the history of the place. They found ut, among other things, that the zoo had been hit by a stray German V-1 buzz bomb during the war, and that some of the dangerus wild animals, such as lions and tigers, had escaped from their amaged cages, creating quite a threat to the people in the town or a period of time. They also went by and saw the famous statue alled "The Pis." It was actually a small water fountain with a tatue of a young boy urinating. It seemed like a strange and omewhat embarrassing thing to have in a prominent place of a ajor city, but the Belgians seemed to be proud of it. Finally, omeone explained to them that somewhere in Belgium's history;

a young prince had wandered off and gotten lost. A tremendous effort was undertaken to search for him, but to no avail. The king finally decreed that if and when the prince was found, he would have a statue made of him doing whatever it was he was doing at that moment—and urinating was what he apparently was doing.

As evening wore on, they went into a café and ran into a couple of guys they knew from the camp. They were sitting with some girls and asked Mark and Walt to join them. Mark soon found himself with a strikingly beautiful girl who spoke fairly fluent English. The next thing he knew, they were all walking down the avenue, arm in arm, to a place that had a good band they could dance to.

Mark could not help noticing the concentration of prostitutes, soliciting their wares on one of the corners they passed on their way.

They reached the dance hall, and had a great time dancing to the small, but lively band. It played American music interspersed with some delightful Belgium numbers. Mark felt that this might be his last fling at bachelorhood before reaching the States and possibly getting married, so he propositioned his date. She quickly indicated that, despite the great time they were having, he would have to pay for her sexual favors.

This was a real blow to his ego and, even though he had the money and was very worked up, he couldn't make himself agree to pay her. He kept trying to woo her during the rest of the evening, but she held firm.

Mark couldn't help but think that this was the difference between a French girl and a Belgian girl. If a French girl is attracted to you and enjoys your company, she'll do it for love. A Belgian girl is more practical and level-headed and, no matter how much she enjoys herself, money is money, and she isn't going to give herself away for nothing.

He finally got discouraged and left the group to catch the bus back to the base. But the beautiful girl had gotten him

notionally very warm. As he walked down the avenue and
ssed the corner where the prostitutes were hanging out, he was
pproached by one of the prettier ones that he remembered seeing
rlier. He agreed to go with her.

Since he had to catch the midnight bus, there was not
uch time to waste, and they made love in her hotel room rather
iickly. As he was getting dressed, he noticed that she was not
aking any effort to dress herself. Instead, she went back over to
e bed and did something that he had never seen a girl do before.
ie masturbated. She rubbed her fingers between her legs, with
r eyes closed. She arched her back as she grew more and more
cited, and then gave a little moan and a shudder as he left the
om.

CHAPTER 52

(Belgium; Troop ship, Atlantic Ocean)

After being at Camp Lucky Strike for a little over a week, Mark's day finally came for boarding a troop ship. There was the usual "hurry up and wait." But the long line he found himself in slowly moved toward the gangplank and up the flimsy ramp onto the ship. Once on board, he located his large, but rather Spartan, room and saw that he would be sharing it with seven other officers.

It was a Liberty Ship, one of hundreds built by Henry Kaiser at the miraculous rate of almost one a day, to move men and materials to and from the war zones. There were none of the finer appointments and niceties that he had experienced in the converted luxury liner that had taken him to combat. Yet, just being on board a ship that would soon be bound for home was a wonderful feeling. He couldn't help but hold his breath until it actually started pulling out of the harbor; for fear that something would happen to keep them from sailing.

Nearly every man went up on deck immediately after finding his bunk, so as to watch the ship pull away from the dock. As they stood there waiting, an announcement burst from the loud speaker.

"Now hear this. Welcome aboard, gentlemen. This is Captain Hansen speaking. We know you are anxious to get home as quickly as possible, and it should be smooth sailing. For tonight's meal, we shall have steak, mashed potatoes and peas, tossed salad, fresh milk, and ice cream."

The cheer was deafening. They had not eaten steak since leaving the States, nor had they had any fresh salad. It was hard to believe how much you could miss a thing like salad after not having any for such a long time.

CHAPTER 53

(Atlantic Ocean)

The journey home was rather uneventful, except for a severe storm they encountered while crossing the notorious North Sea. The ship fought the tormenting waters tirelessly for two days. During the peak of the storm, as he sat down to dinner, Mark noticed that the tablecloth was wet. When he asked the steward about it, he told him that it had been soaked to keep the dishes from sliding off the table as they ate. All during the meal, they could hear the sounds of breaking dishes coming from the kitchen and pantry areas. What a challenging time the cooks and waiters must be having back there. When the ship was hit by one very forceful wave, Mark saw the salt and pepper shakers tip over on the table. He figured that it was probably as far over as he would care to see the ship tilt.

All officers had been assigned a duty of some sort. Mark's was that of "mess checker" for the trip. The idea of having a mess checker was to make sure that the enlisted men didn't go through the chow line twice. Its aim was to ensure that the food didn't run out before everyone got fed. The enlisted men had been given a mess card which he was supposed to punch as they entered the mess hall. His post was at the bottom of the stairs that descended from the outer deck, where the chow line formed. But on stormy days, his duty was really not required, because about a third of the men who descended the stairs got a whiff of the food as they got to the door of the dining room, turned pale, and made a rapid retreat back upstairs, trying to reach the deck railing before throwing up. Even though his card punching was obviously not required on a stormy day, a duty was a duty, and he conscientiously stood there every day, until each and every meal was over.

CHAPTER 54

(USA)

The thrill of pulling into New York Harbor, passing the Statue of Liberty, and being met by a boat loaded with a military band playing patriotic and popular music was overwhelming. There wasn't a throat on board that was not choked up with emotion.

Upon docking, the pilots were taken by train to Fort Dix, New Jersey for further processing.

"Gentlemen, you will be given a thirty-day leave. After your leave, you will report back here for your reassignment to the Pacific. The war there with Japan is still going on hot and heavy."

As soon as he could, Mark got to a phone and put through a call to his home in Wilmington. His mother answered, and she got excited when she heard his voice.

"Mark. Where are you and when are you coming home?"

"Hi, Mom. I'm at Fort Dix, New Jersey, and will be coming home in two days."

"I can't wait to see you. How are you, all right?"

"I'm fine, Mom. Have you heard anything from Joanne?"

"No. I talked to her mother a few weeks ago, and I guess she's going to get married."

The words confirmed Mark's greatest fears and made him shudder. He couldn't believe that he was going to lose the beautiful girl of his dreams.

The next morning there was a heavy overcast. The officers fell out into formation in front of their barracks, awaiting instructions about their pending thirty-day leave. The cloud layer was quite low and produced a slight mist. They suddenly heard the unmistakable roar of the twin engines of a B-25 airplane flying overhead in the overcast at a very low altitude. It could not have been more than a few hundred feet above them. Even though New Jersey was relatively flat, the plane sounded much too low for its safety, and they had the feeling that it was having trouble of some sort. Later that afternoon, they heard on the radio that a B-25 had flown into the Empire State Building.

CHAPTER 55

(Wilmington, Delaware)

Mark left for home by train the next morning with instructions to report back to Fort Dix at the end of thirty days, to be processed for shipment to the Far East.

As the train slowed down, pulling into the station in Wilmington, he looked out the window and was glad to see his mother, Uncle Max, and Aunt Betty waiting for him on the platform. They were accompanied by a nice-looking young girl in her midtwenties whom Mark had never seen before.

He lugged his heavy B-4 bag off the train, plopped it down, and rushed over to give his mother, aunt, and uncle a big hug. His mother said how wonderful it was to have him home, and brushed away a small tear with her finger.

After a few more warm words of elation, his uncle stopped long enough to say, "This is Dorothy Healy. She rents a room from your mother and has been a lot of company for her while you were gone."

Mark shook hands with her and found her demeanor and friendly smile quite attractive.

They loaded his bag into the trunk of the car and drove back to his home in Hillcrest.

One thing he really missed was his father. He had died almost a year earlier, and Mark knew how happy and proud he would have been to welcome him home.

Dorothy Healy turned out to be quite a lively girl with a great sense of humor. She worked as a waitress at the Wilson Hotel. She also mentioned that she had dated some of the pilots at the local army air base.

Mark's home looked good to him as he walked up the stairs of the front porch, through the living room, and plopped his B-4 bag on his bed. It was a three-bedroom bungalow in a middle-class, suburban neighborhood. It bordered woods where he used to take his police dog, Rex, for a walk every day when he got home from high school.

The house furnishings which were bought over the years didn't match very well, but had a certain charm which made a house into a home.

The only thing missing was Joanne.

CHAPTER 56(Wilmington, Delaware)

Mark decided to call Joanne.

He dialed her number and her mother answered.

"Hello, Mark. No, Joanne is not here. Yes, it's true. She's getting married in three days at the Chapel Hills Baptist Church here in Jackson. Yes, he's a very nice young man and they seem to be happy.

"I'm glad to hear that you got home safely. Good-bye, Mark."

Mark spent the rest of the day with his mother and aunt and uncle. They talked about the shortages they had to endure because of the war: gasoline, butter, and sugar. They seemed to avoid talking to Mark about his combat. They probably feared that it would trigger some unpleasant memories that would make him feel uncomfortable.

All of Mark's neighborhood buddies were in the service as well, and he missed not having the chance to chat with them.

The next day, they went to the cemetery and placed a bouquet of flowers on his father's grave. Mark arranged them neatly next to his tombstone and lingered a while, wishing so much he could talk to him.

It was nice to be with his family, but his underlying, recurring thought throughout the day was of Joanne, and the fact that he was going to lose her.

He decided to drive out to Newcastle Air Base to see if there was any chance of catching an available space on a military flight in the direction of Jackson.

He learned that they did have C-47 transport going to Montgomery, Alabama at eight o'clock the next morning and, yes, there was room enough for him to go.

He figured that if he got that far, he might be able to catch a bus the rest of the way to Jackson, Mississippi. Timing was critical, however. The flight might get there too late for him to get a bus leaving the same day. If so, he would have to wait until the next morning and miss the wedding.

CHAPTER 57

(Jackson, Mississippi)

The church was beautifully decorated with flowers and ribbons everywhere. The pews were filled with beautiful people dressed in their "Sunday finest."

The organ was playing soft, melodic music that was peaceful, yet with a hint of more dramatic interludes to come.

Joanne was absolutely stunning in her bridal dress as she started down the aisle.

The organ started playing "Here Comes the Bride."

She was about halfway to the platform when the serenity of the room was shattered by a disturbance at the entrance way.

Everybody tried to ignore it, but the noise got louder.

The organist played her music louder.

Finally, Joanne stopped and turned to see what was causing the commotion.

In the doorway stood Mark, with two men trying to hold him back.

He shouted, "Joanne, no! Not him. Me!"

She stopped, petrified. She turned to look at her husband to be, and then looked back at Mark.

She started to go forward, took three steps, then stopped, and turned to look at Mark again. When their eyes met, she felt a quiver go through her. She felt the power of his magnetism again tugging at her heart. It was the same feeling that drew her to him when she was surrounded by other cadets over a year ago at the SO dance. The feeling blotted out everything else in the room.

She turned and flung her bridal bouquet in the air to her maid of honor, and then ran to Mark.

They embraced passionately, and then ran out the door together.

The End

CPSIA information can be obtained at www.ICGtesting.com
226593LV00001B/1/P